Stiletto to the Pedal

by

Karen C. Whalen

The Tow Truck Murder Mysteries

Cover Art by *Diana Carlile*

The Wild Rose Press, Inc.
PO Box 708
Adams Basin, NY 14410-0708
Visit us at www.thewildrosepress.com

Publishing History
First Edition, 2024
Trade Paperback ISBN 978-1-5092-5453-8
Digital ISBN 978-1-5092-5454-5

The Tow Truck Murder Mysteries
Published in the United States of America

Dedication

Dedication: As always, to Tim

Acknowledgments

There are many people to thank, but foremost is beta reader Sandra Hilger who tells me straight up what works and what doesn't. I appreciate her frankness. Also, I can't imagine getting through the process without the support of fellow writers Rhonda Blackhurst, Pam Wells, and Teri M. Brown. Tow truck expert Amanda Sawyers helps with the technical scenes, but any errors are mine alone. I appreciate my editor at The Wild Rose Press, Ally Robertson, and cover artist, Diana Carlile. And last, a special thanks to my readers.

Chapter 1

My black high-heeled boots rested on the table where I crossed my ankles in satisfaction. Not long ago I'd solved another murder, so I was feeling pretty good about myself. Me, super sleuth and bad-ass tow truck driver.

Yes, you heard that right. But the hardest thing to believe…it's not the super sleuth part, it's the tow truck part.

In my entire twenty-eight years I'd never driven any kind of a truck, let alone a tow truck. Not until I inherited the truck from my absent dad. Then the bodies started piling up. I was still learning to haul cars the hard way, along with solving crime—on the job.

My former boyfriend and mentor, Tanner Utley, had trained me in the car hauling business. My current boyfriend, Sheriff Ephraim Lopez, had warned me off the murder solving business. But I couldn't help it if I stumbled across dead bodies. Killers often stashed their victims in the trunks of cars. And I towed cars. It just seems wrong not to solve the murders, like I was being disrespectful of the dead…and besides, I'm doing my duty as a citizen to look into the crime. Maybe I'm not the best car hauler around town, but I'm not too bad at digging for clues. And maybe my quest for the truth had something to do with my dad's unsolved death, too. My dad's hit-and-run accident was the mystery that haunted me the most.

Leaning back, I admired my boots, rotating my pointed toes first one way, then another, dreaming of investigating a homicide—grim, I know, but fascinating—when the thundering sound of knuckles rapping on wood made my feet crash to the floor like heavy rocks in a mountain slide. The knock wasn't on a door with *Delaney Morran, Private Investigator*, etched in the glass. Not on a door with *Delaney Morran, vehicle recovery specialist,* etched in the glass either. It wasn't even a door. I didn't actually have an office or a desk or a door, only a wood table in my favorite coffee shop, Roasters on the Ridge. This is the place where I sorted out the paperwork and balanced the business account. This is where I waited for my phone to ring for a tow. But there hadn't been any calls this morning, so here I sat. Bored…and daydreaming about investigating crimes in my imaginary office.

The rap of knuckles sounded a second time. I looked up at the man hovering over me. "Yes? May I help you with something?"

"I was told you are Delaney Morran of Del's Towing?" A man ten or so years older than me, maybe pushing forty, wore a plaid bow tie with a white, button-down shirt, a gray sweater vest, black dress pants, and polished wingtips. His brown hair was short and receding. His voice trembled and his Adam's apple bobbed when he spoke. "They told me at the counter that you're Ms. Morran."

"That's me, Delaney. Do you need a tow?" I slammed my laptop shut and slid it inside the case. He looked like a man who could use some assistance. A man who didn't know much about cars. A man not qualified to carry a Man Card. *Yeah-ez!* Bad for him, good for me. This is the part I liked best about my job. I felt a lot of satisfaction when helping people in need…even if I wasn't the best at it.

"No, I don't need a tow." He plonked a black leather portfolio on the table.

Well, bummer. I held my hand up to shade my eyes from the sun that glared through the window behind him. Cold air emanated from the glass. Aspens with new leaves and tall mountain peaks topped with snow dominated the view. It was quite chilly in May in this Colorado mountain town, but spring was in the air and the early morning sun was bright.

I asked him, "Then how can I help you?"

"I'm with the Internal Revenue Collection Office."

I felt the blood rising in my cheeks, and cursed the pale complexion and freckles that went along with the curly red hair I'd braided into a single plait down my back. My nose turned red and I hoped my flush would be mistaken for a bad head cold.

He held out his hand. "I'm Benedict DiNardo, Revenue Officer."

I half-stood and numbly took hold of his hand. He gave mine a half-hearted shake, then let go, and dropped back into my chair. I hadn't completely ignored that worrisome *Balance Due* notice, but I never expected a collection agent to walk in.

He sized me up and his gaze made me squirm. "There's the matter of $1,437.12 owed by Del's Towing per tax code §2.3104.141a."

I rolled my eyes so far back it was like looking in a rearview mirror. "You came in person to collect that? I mean, really?"

"I'm serious, Miss. You are not in compliance with the tax code."

I tossed my hands in the air. "Pffttt. What's the big deal? It's only a thousand bucks." Well, a little bit more than that. When the tax man continued to stare at me, I said, "I'm taking care of it. I gave my accountant all my tax stuff and she's sorting it out."

I may have been bluffing about it not being a big deal. One thousand four hundred crisp ones might as well be one thousand four million because it was just as unattainable for me at the moment.

Breaking news: I had a long way to go in perfecting my tow truck driving skills. I wasn't qualified to carry the Man Card either. My bank account, the one I should have been balancing instead of daydreaming, was at an all-time low. I'm all-girl, petite at five-foot-two, trying to make a living in a man's world, one simple tow at a time. I may have trouble lifting tow dollies and ratcheting chains, but up until this point I thought I'd been doing an okay job handling the business side. I guess not, despite the fact I'd paid my estimated quarterly taxes without the aid of an accountant. So when I received the IRS notice, I asked my mentor Tanner Utley for the name of his bookkeeper and hired her on the spot—she gave me a deep discount for first-time customers. I not only felt like an imposter in the vehicle recovery business, lil' ole me driving a big truck, but I couldn't even get the taxes right. And here I'd honestly thought I might get a little refund, which I was hoping would pay the accountant.

"Here's my card." He placed it on the table with a snap. Benedict DiNardo, IRS Revenue Officer, Collections.

I glanced up for another look at his bobbing Adam's apple and nervous hands. This man was a total a nerd. A dweeb, a real poindexter. His name should be *DiNerdo*. I pressed a hand to my mouth to stop from saying that out loud.

Note to self: Be nice. Don't be rude.

"I'll have my accountant call you," I said, all little Miss Polite.

The owner of the coffee shop, Kristen Guttenberg, sidled up to the table with a steaming carafe in one hand. Around her waist was the café's black apron embroidered with a swirl of steam over a coffee mug. She asked, "Do you need a refill?"

I couldn't answer because the coffee grinder suddenly shrieked with a deafening, pulverizing sound. My eyes darted around and landed on the quaint plaques on the opposite wall that announced, "Coffee makes everything possible" and "Humanity runs on coffee." Antique skis and poles, snowshoes, and ski boots mounted on the other three walls provided a themed ambiance. Distressed-wooden shelves held sacks of beans, rows of mugs, and bottles of syrups. With the deafening grinder pounding away, I couldn't hear the epic, inspiring music that ordinarily played.

This was my happy place, but not so much at the moment.

Quiet reigned when the grinder abruptly came to a halt. Kristen raised her dark eyebrows. "Is everything all right here?" Kristen was my best friend and knew me better than anyone else did. She probably sensed the tension between me and the IRS man.

"Everything's fine." I gave her a look that said *I'll tell you later*.

DiNardo cleared his throat with a loud *harrumph.* "So, you'll have your accountant call me?" He pinned me with a glare.

I tapped the toes of my shoes on the cement floor and felt Kristen's curious eyes on me. "Yes, yes."

"See that she does."

"I will." I had to refrain myself from saluting and saying, *yes sir.* "She'll call you. Her name is Emerald Clark with Spruce Ridge Accounting. I'll get in touch with her right away, Mr. DiNerdo."

"It's DiNardo. Benedict DiNardo." He straightened his bow tie between his thumbs and forefingers.

Omigod. I did a facepalm. "Oops, sorry."

DiNardo lifted his portfolio off the table and tucked it under his arm before heading out. After the door shut behind him with a blast of cool air, I breathed a sigh of relief.

"Well?" Kristen set the carafe on the table and slid into the seat opposite me.

"You know that tax notice I told you about? That man is a collector from the IRS." I brushed the back of my hand across my tight forehead.

Her eyes got big. "No!"

"I wish I was kidding."

We both shuddered. The IRS was the mythical creature we were all afraid of.

"I need to talk to Emerald Clark, my accountant." I half-chuckled. "What kind of a name is Emerald anyway? What were her parents thinking? It reminds me of a witch or the wicked stepsister in a children's movie."

My friend circled her hand in the air. "No, it's like a princess or a mermaid."

That's the difference between Kristen and me. She

always thinks of the good, and me the bad. She is four inches taller and ten times a better person than me and has widely spaced gray eyes, dark shapely brows, and shiny, smooth brown hair. I always wanted her smooth hair. And, to be tall like her. With shiny hair. And she's a purist who roasts her own beans, so I took *half-a-mo* to breathe in the calming smell of the fresh pot. That familiar, comforting aroma was one I was well acquainted with. When Kris opened her shop, Roasters on the Ridge, she asked me to help and I jumped at the chance. I'd only recently made the career change from barista to full-time tow truck driver.

"Well, I hope she's not a mere princess or mermaid. I hope she's a competent accountant." I took a long draw of my tepid coffee and set it back down. "I'd take more of that coffee, but I'm going to head over to her office right now. By this time she's had a chance to look at the thumb drive I gave her."

"I'm sure she'll have it all figured out." Kristen gave my hand a squeeze.

I pushed back my chair and slung my computer bag over my shoulder. Kris made me promise to let her know what the accountant said, then with keys in hand I ducked out the door.

My red tow truck was parked at the far side of the lot.

My Fulcan Xtruder, a self-loader, was the best in the industry. My impressive truck has a tow boom, which looks like a giant crossbar in the shape of a "T", not like a regular old tow truck that has a big hook on the back. My dad's company name, "Del's Towing," the name I'd decided to keep, was painted on the door along with the outline of a black stiletto. I'd added the stiletto to the logo since I was becoming known around my small town as the high-heeled tow truck driver. Yes, I wore heels on the job because that set me apart from the all-male competition. My customers expected me to wear heels when I showed up to tow their cars.

I opened the truck, sat myself down in the front seat, and clasped the steering wheel. A faint smell of motor oil, combined with a woodsy scent, clung to the upholstery, a distinct departure from the coffee shop. I turned the key, the truck came to life, and I pulled out into the stream of traffic, gunning it.

Lights from emergency vehicles lit up the road ahead of me, and I had to slow down. When I finally came alongside the three-story, redbrick building that housed a realtor's office, a dentist, and Spruce Ridge Accounting, I spotted several police cars near the front door, so I angled my truck into the parking lot across the street and hastened over.

Sheriff Ephraim Lopez, in military-fit shape and a pressed, light blue uniform, spoke to a couple other officers milling around the doorway. I hung on the periphery but couldn't catch their words. Something bad had most certainly gone down, but what? There was no smoke coming from any windows, no scorch marks on the building. No armed robber being manhandled into the back of a police cruiser. Nobody giving an injured person CPR.

Note to self: Listen to your police scanner so you know what's going on around town.

Ephraim glanced my way and I caught his eye. He nodded, so I remained where I was, waiting for him to have a free moment. I played with the screensaver on my phone, exchanging the background photo of a famous brand stiletto for another with red-soled heels.

After about ten long minutes, Ephraim headed in my direction.

My boyfriend was five-foot-eleven and had the bronze complexion of his Mexican heritage, with dark brown eyes and hair. His uniform affirmed serious muscles underneath. He's a good sheriff who didn't mind my curiosity. For the most part, anyway.

"Delaney, what are you doing here?" He hooked an arm around my neck, pulling me toward him. Then he gave a quick kiss to the top of my head and let go of me. I caught a whiff of his aftershave, citrus, jasmine, and musk—clean and fresh and appealing.

"I need to see my accountant. She's in this building." I jerked my thumb in the direction of the crowded doorway.

The smile froze on his face. "What's your accountant's name?"

"Emerald Clark."

His eyes widened for a second, then his face shuttered.

I asked, "What happened here?" The creases deepened in his forehead. "Ephraim, tell me." I wasn't just a nosy bystander anymore.

His hands dropped to his sides. "There's been a homicide."

Another murder!

It had happened again.

Here in Spruce Ridge.

This small town served as the gateway to the Rocky Mountains and Colorado ski areas…a desirable and affluent location between Denver and Vail that normally had very little crime until this recent spate of murders.

At least this time I didn't find the body, and Ephraim had to be glad about that. This death had nothing to do with the towing business or with me. But that didn't keep my stomach from flip-flopping.

The group of officers broke apart and two paramedics pushed a stretcher on wheels through them to an open ambulance. A body was covered by a blanket, except for the feet, one bare foot and one high-heeled foot. I'd know that crisscross strap sandal in black leather anywhere.

I stared in open-mouthed astonishment and blinked away the tears that threatened to well up. "No." *Lord, no.*

Ephraim wrapped his arms around me and I buried my face against his chest. "Are you going to be all right, Delaney?"

His height forced me to tilt my head backwards to look up at him. This lawman had a job to do and I didn't want to keep him from doing it. I assured him, "Sure. I'm good." *Right! When pigs fly.*

"I need to get back over there. We're securing the scene." He gestured toward the office building. I let go of him and he strode across the lot to join the other deputies.

I tottered to the side of the building in my heeled boots and braced myself against the cold, hard bricks.

My accountant was dead.

Emerald Clark had an unusual name, had been a pretty brunette about my age, and had worn nice shoes. That's the sum total of what I knew about her. Since Ephraim said it was a homicide, her office was a crime scene. The forensic team was probably inside right now going over everything for fingerprints and hair samples, taking her computer and files into custody, looking for clues. All access would be denied and her office cordoned off with yellow crime scene tape.

The flash drive with my records was somewhere with all that evidence. What was I going to do about that pesky tax bill now?

I looked over my shoulder, half expecting Benedict DiNardo, IRS Revenue Officer, to be standing there, one hand fiddling with his bow tie, the other hand stretched out for the money I owed.

All I could think about was my little problem with the IRS.

That's how self-centered I am. I'm so bad.

Chapter 2

My cell rang. The woman on the other end said, "I need a tow," and the vehicle recovery side of my brain clicked in.

"What kind of car and what's your location?" I couldn't let gloomy thoughts about Emerald Clark's death, or even lame worries about my silly tax bill, stop me. I needed to toughen up and get back to work.

When the customer gave me the info, I climbed into my truck, cranked the engine, and sped off toward the older part of town. I cruised along Main Street, quaint and touristy with expensive boutiques and breweries, plus a coffee shop that rivaled Kristen's. Then I left-turned at Columbine Court and pulled up to a Toyota RAV4.

Front-wheel drive is standard in this model, but all-wheel drive is optional, so I asked the driver which it was. All wheel.

All right, then.

This was the part I liked best. This was when the magic happened. This was what made my job fun. You see, my self-loader has an integrated hydraulic wheel-lift system—pretty slick—operated by a wireless remote. With a push of the button, the giant T-bar lowered to the ground, and metal hooks, called "claws," grabbed the vehicle's tires. After the claws were engaged, I crouched down in my heels to release the tow dollies from under the truck bed. Once I unhooked the clips, the heavy dollies rolled out. I positioned the first set around the front passenger tire and jacked the wheel up with the foot pedal. I did the same on the front driver's side.

The woman dogged my steps. "Do you need me to put my car in neutral?"

"No, I don't. Step back. Please."

Here's the deal when towing, if the target vehicle is front-wheel drive, the front wheels need to be lifted off the ground, if rear-wheel drive, the rear wheels need to be lifted, and if all-wheel, as in this case, all four wheels have to be raised. The car does not need to be in neutral.

I hit the button on the remote, my truck went through all the motions, and the back of the Toyota swung into the air. My dollies had raised the front of the car and the hydraulic lift had elevated the back.

Cool, huh?

But when I explained how it worked to my customer, she said, "It doesn't need to be in neutral? I don't get it."

"It took me a while at first to understand it, too," I said. "Just trust me." I gave my truck a pat. I was all set to ask her where she wanted me to take her Toyota, when another tow truck pulled in alongside us.

I almost groaned out loud. It was Owen Eckerd, my competition, a tow operator who drove the butt-ugliest green tow truck you ever saw. His was a wrecker with the big hook on the back. Owen's color blindness explains why he always wears orange and drives a green truck, but doesn't explain his long beard.

The customer ran over to Owen's open window and said, "Can you tow my car?"

I said, "Excuse me?"

13

She turned back to me. "I'd prefer this man handle the tow."

"What?" My face scorched hot.

I gave Owen the *do-something!* look, but he smiled at the woman and said, "Of course."

It was the unspoken law in the car hauling business that the first tow driver on the scene got the job. And she'd called *me* for the tow. And what stunk worse than burnt espresso beans…this wasn't the first time Owen had taken a job away from me.

I opened my mouth to defend myself, but I could barely pull air into my lungs.

The customer said, "Sorry, but I'm giving the job to him."

Did this woman prefer a male over a female driver? A slow burn filled my chest because it wasn't the first time this kind of thing had happened to me. Some customers, ones who didn't know me, were surprised when a woman responded to their call—surprised that Del was female. They must not have heard about my high-heeled reputation. Women like this one weren't the only customers to have an issue with a female tow truck driver. Men did, too. In fact, it was mostly the men. Men especially hated it when they'd run out of gas or had a flat tire, like they should be able to manage a simple problem themselves and not need a woman to fix it for them. Sure, I was a female competing in a typically male job, but I was fiercely proud of being a woman—a highly competitive woman—in a man's world. Which was one of the reasons I flaunted the high heels on my logo and on my feet. I was not about to concede that a man could do a better job hauling cars.

Because I could do it.

Or, at least I should get points for trying harder than anyone else.

Owen climbed out of his cab. He was wearing what must be his favorite orange football jersey since I'd seen him in it before. His shirt barely contained his belly; he was obviously a well-fed man. The tight silver band that encircled his plump wrist was stamped with the snake-stick symbol, and I wondered if his color-blindness warranted a medical alert bracelet.

"Owen?" I gave him the death-ray stare as if to say *back-off*.

He told me, "Lower the Toyota, Delaney."

You're not the boss of me! I didn't actually say that out loud in front of the customer.

Just act cool. I'm cool, I'm cool, I told myself as I hit the button and lowered the woman's vehicle. The rear tires hit the ground with a soft *pumpf*, the claws retracted, and the crossbar folded back onto the truck bed with a final squeak. At least Owen helped me trundle my tow dollies back into my truck's undermounts.

"I could charge you a drop fee," I said to the woman, but she only waved her hand in dismissal. It's a good thing I was accustomed to humiliation.

Back in my truck, I waited until Owen left the scene with the woman and her Toyota, then I slammed my palms into the steering wheel five or six times.

Frustrated, much?

But the customer was always right and she had the option to choose who towed her vehicle.

But Owen Eckerd should've insisted I handle the tow.

How could I get even with that Owen Eckerd?

I fantasized about accepting an award for *Tow Truck*

Driver of the Year as Owen looked on. In my mind I lifted a hefty statuette into the air like a world cup winner and smiled as the audience cheered. Then I wondered if there was such an award and how I could find out about it. I'd have a long way to go to be a contender, but one could dream. Those thoughts occupied my brain as I drove over to Oberly Motors.

The key fob chirped when I locked my truck behind the secure fence in the corner of the autobody shop's parking lot, then I turned and strode through the first of three auto bays. The blasting sound of an air compressor and pungent paint fumes shot out the door. When he spotted me, Byron Oberly, stocky and in his fifties, turned the paint sprayer off and lowered his safety glasses. Red paint marked his blue coveralls and black grease caked the cracks in his calloused hands.

He smiled with his gap-toothed grin. "How ya' doin', Delaney?" His deep voice reverberated through the garage.

"Hey, Old Man."

That's what I called Byron Oberly. He'd never been married, as far as I knew, and didn't have any kids of his own, but his nieces and nephews called him, "Old Man," so I did, too. He was the one who'd bought my dad's autobody business after his death and had changed the name from "Del's Motors" to "Oberly Motors." I had inherited the truck. Byron Oberly had purchased the shop. And he'd hired my roommate Axle, a naturally talented mechanic, and let me park my truck at his lot. So every morning when I took Axle to work, I also picked up my truck, and when I dropped the truck off at the end of the day, I picked up Axle. Worked out pretty well for everybody.

I scraped out a folding chair with dirty rags hung over the back and gingerly took the edge of the seat, sitting forward. "Where's Axle?"

"He's cleanin' up in the washroom. I'm just finishin' this job, then I'm done for the day, too."

"Who's your accountant, Byron?" A breeze blew in through the open garage door, ruffling the loose strands that escaped my braid. There was a bite in the air hinting that summer was still a month away.

"Spruce Ridge Accountin'." He pulled a red rag from a pocket and wiped his forehead.

"Yeah, that's mine, too." Small town. I didn't know any other accounting firms in the area. "You heard Emerald Clark was killed today?"

He splayed one hand across his chest. "Who's she?"

I gave him a questioning look. "The accountant at Spruce Ridge Accounting."

He *tsked* and shook his head. "The one I use is Megan Putnam. She's the one that keeps my books."

"Oh, I didn't realize there were two in that office. Are there others?" When I'd met Clark, she'd walked me back from an empty lobby to her private office and shut the door. I didn't see any other employees.

"I don't know." He shrugged. "So, what happened?"

"Well, I went over to see Clark, and when I got there the sheriffs had the building cordoned off, so I stopped and talked to Ephraim, then the paramedics brought her body out on a stretcher. Ephraim said it's homicide. I don't know how she was killed, though."

Byron nodded, his lips turned down. "That's awful."

"I know. Very sad." But I didn't really know her. And I couldn't help but wonder if the other accountant in Clark's office could help me with the IRS. That thought cheered me a little.

Axle stopped in the lobby doorway and rested one hand on either side of the frame. My roommate was Kristen's eighteen-year old cousin who moved into my spare room to help me out with the rent. As a male teen, he wasn't home a lot, an easy roomie, although he was a typical teenager with an attitude, doing stupid teenager things that occasionally caused me to worry about him. And he'd brought his Rottweiler with him, so I now had a dog, too. Today he wore his usual oversized sneakers, baggy pants, sweatshirt with the logo of an Indie band on the front, and dirty knit cap. He had Kristen's same gray eyes, black eyebrows, and dark hair.

Byron told him, "Delaney was just sayin' how there's another murder."

Axle cast his gaze in my direction. "Are you frickin' kidding me?"

I put a little sarcasm in my voice. "*Ohhhh yeah*, I joke about stuff like this all the time, lil' cuz." That's what I called him.

"Really? Jeez, Delaney. Not funny." Axle, may be a great mechanic aptly named, but his brain wasn't fully in gear at the moment.

"I'm kidding!"

"I get it!" He popped his eyes wide like a teenager in a sulk.

"No, you don't." I let out a half-hearted laugh.

He shot me an accusatory look. "You're one sick chick."

I held up my hand, palm out. "Stop. Just stop. Push the reset button. There really is another murder. My accountant, Emerald Clark. I wasn't joking about that."

"Oh. Don't know her, but that sucks." He gave me

an awkward back pat.

I agreed, "Yeah, it blows."

He plugged a wireless earbud into one ear and messed with his phone. He didn't know the victim; he wasn't affected by her death. He had the attitude of the young, believing bad things only happened to someone else. But I couldn't blame him. All I could think about was how her death complicated my problems with the IRS. He slid his phone into a pocket and his earbud blared so loudly I'm sure I could hear the rap music as well as he could.

I gave Axle a push. "Ready to go home?"

He gave me a head nod and mock-punched me on the arm.

We piled into my silver Fiat 500, a cute Italian job something like a Smart Car. Five minutes later we were at Pine Street and Eagle Avenue where Roasters on the Ridge sat on the corner.

I locked the Fiat and Axle stepped aside so I could proceed him up the outside staircase to the second floor above the coffee shop. Kristen had the apartment across the landing from ours. I loved living with my friend so close. Just a quick couple of steps away and I could talk to Kris anytime. It was also convenient to the coffee shop below. *Win-win.*

My door opened to the kitchen where I'd squeezed in a tiny table, and beyond that was a compact living room with a pair of facing loveseats, then a hall leading to two bedrooms and one bath. Axle's Rottweiler, named Boss, galloped toward us and jumped up on Axle's knees. I gave the little monster two treats from the biscuit bag and he gulped them down.

Axle slouched into the couch and kicked off his

shoes, while Boss arranged himself on the cushions. The word art on the wall spelled out, "Family," and the mismatched floral pillows on the loveseats shouted out "shabby chic." The living room window faced the parking lot, but also afforded a view of the ever present pines and snowcapped mountain peaks in the distance.

"You doing all right, Delaney?" Axle clicked on the TV remote. "Want me to ride along with you tonight?" He might be a teenage goofball, but he was also a good wingman. Sometimes he came with me on tows, handy when the phone rang in the middle of the night and I didn't want to go out by myself. "You spooked by another murder?"

"Yeah, maybe a little bit. Would you mind?" I relaxed some, since I'd be glad for the company.

"Nah, but you'll owe me one."

"Hardly. I paid that back."

"Did not."

"Did so." I chuffed him on the side of his head at the same time a knock sounded on the door. I went over and opened it to Kristen.

"Well, what did your accountant say?" She stepped inside and tossed her purse on the kitchen table.

"She's not talkin'," Axle said from the living room, only a few feet away.

"What?" Kristen squinted at her cousin.

"She's toes up, DOA," he answered.

I explained, "Emerald's been killed. Don't ask me how, I don't know that part. All I know is, when I got to her office they were carrying her out on a stretcher."

"Told ya." Axle flicked off the TV and joined us in the kitchen, Boss padding along behind him. Axle leaned his elbows on the counter and stared at me and Kris, actually looking interested for once.

"Killed, what do you mean killed?" Kristen placed a hand over her heart, and when I explained about my accountant's sheet-covered body, she gave me a *pew-eew* face. "What are you going to do now?"

"I don't know. That nerdy tax collector's not going to be happy. I told him my accountant would call him, and that won't happen now." My gaze went to my laptop resting on the counter. "I gave Emerald a flash drive with all my records on it, and I'll need to get that back. Maybe the other accountant in her office can help me, but if not I guess I'll need to find a new accountant. I'll have to put DiNardo off for a while. He'll just have to understand."

Kris wrapped an arm around my shoulder and gave me a light squeeze before letting go. "You can handle that tax guy, Delaney. Just stand up to him. Don't let him intimidate you. That's what they do, you know, use intimidation tactics."

Yeah, well, that egghead *DiNerdo* had to take a number behind the brawny, all-male towers in town, like that mean Owen Eckerd with the butt-ugly green truck.

"Wait." Axle pulled his hand down his face. "You didn't keep a copy of your records?"

"Well, I have all my printed receipts, but I spent hours scanning and organizing them into folders on the thumb drive. I entered everything into a spreadsheet on that drive. I don't want to recreate it all over again, so I need it back."

Axle exchanged a glance with Kristen that said *can you believe this?*

Kristen said, "You didn't keep a copy of the drive?"

"No?" My voice came out high like I was asking a question.

Kristen rubbed my arm. "Talk to Ephraim, see if he'll go into her office and look for it."

"Right." *Wrong.* I thought of the off-limits crime scene and my boyfriend, the cowboy sheriff with the strong moral principles. He did everything by the book. And our relationship was new enough that I didn't want to ask any favors, especially one that would require him to overstep some letter of the law.

"How did you choose this accountant anyway?" Kristen asked.

"She was Tanner's accountant. And I don't know of another local accounting firm." I trusted my former boyfriend and fellow tow truck driver to know the best one for our type of business. "Plus, I found her business card with my dad's stuff and figured he may have used her, too."

Kristen's gray eyes widened slightly. "Your dad?"

I yanked the band from my braid and raked my fingers through my hair while the two of them exchanged another long look. My friends knew how I felt about my dad.

I never knew him. After my parents divorced when I was seven, I never saw him again. Not only was his fatal car accident a mystery, but why he left me his tow truck in his will was mind boggling, too. The man who fathered me had given me his name and his Irish red hair and most recently his self-loader, but no fond memories. I didn't have cool pictures of him teaching me how to ride a bike or drive a car or shoot baskets or any other special moments captured on camera like I imagined every other kid had but me. His death robbed me of the chance to know him, and I was sad for what might have been. That little-girl-lost had hoped to get to know her father, but now it was too late.

So, I was left with trying to make a success of my dad's business, *trying* being the operative word here. I'd retained the business name, "Del's Towing," and told everyone it was for continuity and name recognition, but the truth is, I liked it when customers called me "Del." Like my dad.

Glancing at the kitchen clock, I said, "Anyone hungry? Want to grab a bite?"

"No, thanks, I'm meeting Zach for dinner. See you guys later." Kristen grabbed her purse and pushed out the door. Kristen and Zachariah Bowers, a Spruce Ridge Police officer, were almost engaged.

I asked, "You ready, Ax? I'll buy chili dogs and milkshakes."

"Give me a minute." Axle topped up Boss's food and water bowls, then attached the leash to take his dog for a walk.

Ridgeside Condominium Association had recently hired me to haul non-resident vehicles from their parking lot, but tonight I was working towaway zones for Tanner Utley under his contract with several Main Street businesses. I covered Tuesdays and Thursdays and he handled the rest of the week. Today was Tuesday. Sometimes I towed three or four vehicles a night, generating a big piece of my income.

I went to my closet to change out of my heeled boots into the cute, female version of a man's yellow work boot with flat, heavy soles. Normally when on calls I kept up my image of the high-heeled tow truck operator, but I dealt with a different kind of customer when monitoring the towaway zones, the type who wanted to avoid paying a parking meter. None of them would ever call me out on a job or give me a good review. Nobody liked having their car impounded, even if it was their own fault for ignoring the no-parking signs and blocking the loading docks. Some people even got over-the-top angry. Hence the yellow work boots. Forget the high heels when dealing with those hot heads. They didn't deserve to see me in cute shoes and I could run faster in boots.

Pepper spray—what's in every female vehicle recovery agent's pocket—helped, too.

But, when we finally arrived at the no-parking zones, they were free of illegally parked vehicles. I stationed the truck at the end of the alley and we munched on the hotdogs we'd picked up at the root beer stand.

Axle bobbed his head and tapped his fingers on the dash, listening to his music, and I played solitaire on my phone. An athletic-looking woman with short, cropped hair and a spiderweb tattoo on her neck came out from the back of the sporting goods store. Her tee shirt was emblazoned with the message, *When under attack, counter attack*. I thought she might have stepped outside to smoke a cigarette, but she brought a cell phone up to her ear and started talking, so I went back to my game.

Just then an oversized, black tow truck turned into the alley and stopped alongside us. Another self-loader like my own Fulcan Xtruder. The black truck had dark tinted windows, but I knew who was behind the glass.

I buzzed my window down. "Tanner? What are you doing here? It's my night to work."

He poked his head out his window. His skin looked almost green with his dark blond hair and light brown five o-clock shadow. A sheen of perspiration glistened on his forehead.

"Is everything okay?" I asked him.

"No."

"What's the matter?"

"The cops think I killed Emery!"

Chapter 3

"The cops think I did it." Tanner slammed his truck into park and slouched down in his seat, his shoulders concaved.

I climbed down from my cab, and Axle joined me at Tanner's door. The woman with the spiderweb tattoo gave us a curious look before disappearing inside the sporting goods store. My gaze took in the length of the alley, but it was now deserted except for the three of us.

"Why do they suspect you?" I asked, my voice calm. There had to be a misunderstanding, that's all.

Tanner Utley is an ambitious, self-made man with a Business degree from night school, who built up his towing company from scratch at a young age and who is singlehandedly raising his two younger siblings. His strength and capability are rock solid, like an immovable mountain, and it was hard to see him panicked like this.

He wiped the sweat from his brow with the back of his hand, and his sleeve dropped to reveal multiple ink jobs—a geometric pattern, a bald eagle on a pine tree, and music lyrics. Did I mention he's six-foot tall and good-looking, a head-turner of a tow man?

He said, "Emery was skimming and I knew about it."

"Okay…first thing, Emery is Emerald Clark, right?" When he nodded, I asked, "What do you mean, skimming? Skimming what?"

Axle snorted next to me. "Money, Delaney. She was taking cash off the top."

I stared at Axle. How did this immature eighteen-year old, who might be a mechanical genius but has no common sense, know about such things? Never mind. Don't answer that. I don't want to know.

"Emerald, I mean, Emery, was stealing from her clients?" I asked Tanner. His chin bobbed. "How do you know about this?"

"I noticed it last week on my end-of-month profit report."

And I entrusted her with my bank account information. And my social security number. And she stole from Tanner. *Yikes.*

Note to self: Check bank account balance.

Who was I kidding? There was nothing in my bank account to check.

I said, "I don't see why the police suspect you." Even if his accountant was stealing from him, Tanner would never take her life. He wouldn't kill anyone for any reason. This man wasn't capable of murder.

"I reported her to the sheriff's department." Tanner turned the ignition key and the engine went silent.

"You recommended her to me. Why didn't you let me know about this?" My voice rose an octave.

"Sorry, Delaney. I didn't want to spread it around until they investigated her. What if I'm wrong?"

I crossed my arms over my chest. "Okay. So, the police figure you had a motive. But you can't be the only one."

His shoulders drooped even more. "No one else made a complaint."

Axle chimed in, "It would be stupid for the killer to

report her. A killer wouldn't alert the cops and then go kill somebody. *Duh*. Arrow pointing to chest."

"That's what I thought, too, but the sheriff doesn't agree." Tanner's voice was flat. He rested his forearms over the top of his steering wheel and stared out the windshield.

"It's early yet. The police have just started and they'll discover the truth, you'll see. Was it Ephraim who questioned you?"

"No, some other sheriff." Tanner turned to look me in the eye. "Can you talk to Ephraim? Tell him I didn't do this?"

"Of course." I felt Axle shifting his stance next to me. "I'll find out what the sheriffs know. They have to be looking at other suspects, I'm certain. You'll get past this, Tanner." I forced my words to sound like Kristen's. She was always positive and encouraging and a good example to follow.

Axle poked me in the side and pointed to his watch. "We could get going now. Look at the time."

I threw Tanner an uncertain glance, but he nodded and said. "I need to get home, too. Thanks, Delaney. Let me know what you find out." He turned over the engine and put his truck in gear.

"I will," I said a little too forcefully. Axle tugged on my arm and I followed him the few steps back to my truck.

Once we were in our seats and buckled up, Axle said, "Do you really want to get involved in another murder investigation, Delaney?" I stared at Axle's profile. He said, "You've gotten yourself into some bad shit before. Think about it. You want to do that again?" He rubbed his wireless earbud between his fingers before popping it in his right ear.

"You worried about me?" I asked him.

He gave me a miniscule shrug. "Hey, what do you know?"

"You *are* worried about me, lil' cuz'. I think it's sweet." I pinched my lips together to hold back a wide smile.

He held up a palm. "Barf at the thought."

I gave his fingers a shake. "Tanner's my friend, all right? And it won't hurt for me to talk to Ephraim. I would anyway."

"Ha. You won't stop there, that's the problem. Whatever you do, be careful." He withdrew his hand to insert his left earbud, and with both buds in he tapped on his phone, turning up the music.

I took a moment to bask in the safety and warmth of the truck before starting the motor. The dark night was still and cool outside the cab, and low, white clouds reflected the late evening moonlight. That Axle cared warmed my heart. He and Kristen were like family, like the sister and brother I never had—even though I called him lil' cuz'. But Tanner was important to me, too, and I wasn't going to abandon him.

****

The next morning, Axle and I stopped downstairs at Roasters for coffees to go. When we were headed out the door with our drinks, we ran into that nerdy IRS guy coming in.

"Good morning, Ms. Morran." He held the door open for us.

"Hello DiNerd…*er*…DiNardo." I shot him a sidelong look and kept going.

"One moment. I came here to speak to you." He

29

turned and followed us out. "Your accountant did not call me. I didn't hear from anyone at Spruce Ridge Accounting."

I said, "Something happened. There's been a delay…uh…I'm not sure when I can get the information."

Axle's eyebrows pinched together and he stepped closer to my side. He volunteered, "Delaney's accountant is dead."

"Dead?" DiNardo's Adam's apple bobbed.

I flicked an irritated glance at Axle, then said, "Yes, she died suddenly, but I'm in the process of getting another accountant on board, and I'll get you an answer real soon." Not a total fib. Emerald did die suddenly and I was planning on getting a new accountant, today if possible.

He didn't hesitate. "You still owe $1,437.12 per tax code §2.3104.141a."

"I heard you the first time."

"You have seven days to get your tax status in compliance." He adjusted his bow tie.

"Seven days?" I huffed out a big breath and protested, "There's no way I owe that much. I didn't make a whole lot of money last year. Isn't there a limit to how much taxes I have to pay?"

"You need to take that up with Appeals. I'm with Collections."

"I will." I spun around and stomped toward my Fiat. I felt DiNardo's gaze sear into my back, but didn't give him another glance. Axle folded himself into the passenger seat while I scrambled into the driver's side. Stiletto to the pedal, I careened out of the lot and went from zero to thirty in five seconds, the engine giving off a shrill whine and a couple of shudders. I was really letting DiNardo get to me.

"I'm sorry you owe that man taxes," Axle said in a kind voice.

Awww. His sympathy squeezed at my heart. Spotting a police car partially hidden by a curve in the road, I eased off the gas. "Thanks, Ax, but I don't owe him, I owe the government, and I'm afraid there's no arguing with the government."

"Why not just pony up? He gave you a week deadline. That's not much time."

"It's the principle of the thing." Plus, my bank account. Zero. "I'm going to try reaching the other accountant in Clark's office. In fact, I'll call her right now." I hit blue-tooth and said, "Call Spruce Ridge Accounting." Axle braced himself on the dash when I swung wide at the next corner. But no one picked up my call and I had to leave a message. Since Byron Oberly had told me Megan Putnam was the other accountant, I asked specifically for Megan to call me, saying it was urgent.

Axle tumbled out of the Fiat at Oberly Motors, said a quick goodbye, and made a dash inside. I traipsed up to where I'd stored my self-loader last night and pulled myself into the cab, then cruised over to Front Street and the redbrick structure that housed the accounting office. I was too wired to wait for Megan to call me back. I needed some reassurance right now.

Once inside the building, I climbed the stairs to the third floor and tried the door. Locked. I marshalled my anxious thoughts, told myself to be patient, and retraced my steps back down to my truck.

The Clear Creek County Sheriff's office was in a

modern building, with big windows and lots of natural light, located on the highway leading out of town, and that's where I headed next. I asked the duty clerk for Sheriff Ephraim Lopez. In less than a minute, he came out to take me back to his office with his messy desk, a swivel chair, and two visitors' chairs. I plopped into one of the visitors' chairs.

"I'm glad to see you, but you never come by the station without a reason." He smiled, showcasing his dimples.

Time for the favor. My boyfriend paid strict attention to police procedure, but *whatever*, I had to ask anyway. "I need something out of the accounting office. A thumb drive with my business records on it." I conjured up a hopeful smile.

"The crime scene hasn't been released yet. Forensics is still going over everything. I can't take anything from her office."

Not unexpected. His gaze rested on my fingers raking through the end of my braid, and I quickly let go of the strands. No way I wanted to admit to the sheriff that the IRS was after me. Our relationship was new and discussing money would be cringey-embarrassing.

I asked, "Did you bring Emery's computer back here? Maybe my thumb drive is with it?"

His dark eyebrows climbed up his forehead. "Emery, is it now?"

"Her nickname." I fidgeted in my chair.

"Only her friends called her that."

"Right, well, I heard someone call her Emery." When Ephraim locked onto me with his brown eyes, I admitted, "It was Tanner. Tanner said she went by Emery."

Ephraim's expression hardened into his cop-face. "It's obvious he was close to the victim."

Uh-oh. Did I just make things worse for Tanner?

He asked, "When did you talk to Tanner about Emerald Clark?"

"Last night when I was covering the towaway zones." I clenched my fingers tight in my lap and stared hard at the sheriff. "Why in the world would you ever suspect Tanner of murder? What do you have on him?"

"I can't discuss Tanner with you, especially since you know him so well." He looked as if he was weighing his next words. "I love to talk to you about my work. I appreciate your insight and your intuition and your compassion for victims, but Delaney, I just can't comment on Tanner."

"I understand." *Not!* "Can you tell me how she died? Was she shot or something?"

"It'll be in the newspaper tomorrow, so I can tell you now that she fell down a concrete stairwell. Her neck was broken."

"Oh." The image hit my brain and I blinked at the tears simmering behind my eyes. I had climbed the stairs to the accounting office before I'd come here to the sheriff station. Was that where Emery, *err*, Emerald, died? There was no crime scene tape around the staircase. I suppressed a shudder and asked, "Is that concrete stairwell the one next to the elevator when you come in?"

"No, there are two sets of stairs. She fell down the stairs at the back of the building, not at the front. You can get to both stairwells from the lobby. The front stairs are still open to the public, but the back staircase is closed for now."

I swallowed a lump in my throat. "Are you sure it's homicide? She didn't just slip on the steps?"

He leaned back in his seat, causing the chair to creak. "From the trajectory of the fall it looks like she was pushed pretty hard."

Pushed. Hard. That added an extra layer of depression to the already upsetting image in my mind. My eyes pricked with stinging needles and I blinked them away. "What about time of death? Who found her?"

"She died sometime Monday night, discovered by her business partner Tuesday morning."

"You can't be more precise on the time?"

"That will be made public later, not yet. That's all I can tell you." His voice was stern and his expression no-nonsense, brooking no argument.

We gave each other tense looks. Time to change the subject. For now. I took a moment to calm myself then said, "All right. So, will you let me know when I can get my flash drive back?"

"It's up to forensics to release the scene, and I need to stay out of their way. But I'll ask. How soon do you need it?"

"Like yesterday."

His brown eyes softened. "Okay."

I stood up, and he rose, too. I tagged along after him down the hall to the reception area. He walked me outside to my truck which took up two spaces in the parking lot. As I unlocked the door he stood close to me, and I got a rush.

"See you later tonight?" he asked, placing a hand on my arm.

"Sounds good."

He gently brushed his lips against mine, and his hand lingered on my shoulder, then slid down to my elbow, giving me goosebumps. His eyes strayed to my shoes, the two-tone, brown and tan pumps I was wearing today, because when I left home this morning I was feeling professional, but now not so much. He planted another kiss on my lips, and I returned the kiss. I gave out a sigh as he turned and disappeared into the sheriff's station.

I climbed into my cab, pulled onto the highway, and aimed my truck toward town.

Would the crime scene be released in seven days, the deadline DiNerdo had given me? Surely forensics wouldn't take that long, but what if they did? What if it took too long to get my flash drive back? What if Megan Putnam didn't call me and I needed to find another accountant? Worst case scenario, what if I needed to recreate everything on the drive *and* get a new accountant? Paperwork was my least favorite part of the job.

I turned off on a side road and brought my truck to a stop to call my stepdad. Will would probably tell me to pay the IRS bill, but maybe he wouldn't and it would be nice to get his take on it. Will Sharpton was an undistinguished attorney in a mediocre law firm in Denver that practiced family law, but since my stepdad's goal was to make my mom happy and me independent, he was always willing to help me to that end. After my call was transferred to him through the firm's receptionist, Will picked up.

"I have a favor to ask," I told him.

"What do you need, Laney?"

"You can't tell Mom about this."

"What happened?" Alarm sounded in his voice.

I rushed to explain, "It's no big deal. It seems I owe some money to the IRS. I need to put them off while I get my records together." No reason to bring up that nasty, nerdy tax collector. Or my poor record retention practices. Or the homicide.

"How much do you owe?"

"A bit over a thousand dollars per tax code 2.3 something-something." My pulse revved up a notch just saying that out loud.

"We can lend you the money, you know that."

The *abso-freaking-lutely* last thing I wanted to do was borrow money from my parents. I'd never hear the end of it from my mother, who would lecture me about getting a better paying job. Of course, the *abso-freaking-lutely* next to last thing I wanted to do was owe the government money. I weighed which would be worse, Mom nagging me or the government nagging me.

I said, "Thanks for the offer, but can I get some kind of time extension? Just until I get my paperwork in order. Besides, I really don't think I owe the IRS that much. I think there's some kind of mistake."

"The IRS doesn't usually make mistakes, but you can always ask for more time to pay and even get on a payment schedule, one you can afford."

"I can do that?"

"Sure, sure." His voice sounded so untroubled, it made me feel much more relaxed, too. "They're not always real understanding, but yes, we can give that a try."

"Not understanding?" That relaxed feeling? Gone! I made a tiny noise in the back of my throat. "What do you mean, not understanding?"

"The IRS charges interest on the amount owed. They can put a lien on your accounts, levy your assets, and other remedies, but let's not get ahead of ourselves. I doubt your tax debt is high enough for those drastic measures. I assume you received a notice of some kind?"

"I did."

"I'll need a copy so I can get the case number."

"Right, right." Things were looking up again. Will would get me an extension; it would all work out. "I just need to scan it, then I'll email you the late notice."

"Late? What do you mean, *late* notice? This tax isn't just due, it's overdue?"

"They said I didn't pay enough estimated quarterly taxes. But I thought I overestimated. I swear I did." I threw a hand in the air. "I don't understand how I owe them, Will. That's why I don't want to just roll over and pay it."

"Okay, email me what you have."

I thanked him and we disconnected.

I didn't have a scanner, so I made a beeline to the coffee shop to use Kristen's. Because Kristen was busy with customers, I didn't stop to chat, but made my way to her office and quickly scanned and forwarded the late notice, embarrassingly marked *third late notice*, to Will.

After that, I climbed the stairs to my apartment, unlocked the door and went inside. I hauled out the large cardboard box from the bottom of my closet where I'd tossed the receipts for gasoline, a tune-up, new oil filter, business cards, and the like, but mostly gas—a whole year's worth. I hefted the box onto the kitchen table and opened my laptop. It had taken me days to scan all of the receipts onto the thumb drive for the accountant. Unfortunately, I'd just thrown the tiny receipts and bits of paper into the big box after scanning them. The box was a mess, and it felt like a mountain of paperwork to tackle all over again.

How did I not make an extra copy of the drive? Why didn't I organize the carton of papers into file folders? How could I be that incompetent?

It was only too easy.

And that little memory stick with everything neatly organized was probably bouncing around somewhere in the bottom of a police evidence box, lost in a black hole.

I drubbed a fist to my forehead. If I had that stupid, frickin' drive, my life would be so much easier. I really didn't want to recreate the wheel, but I might have to, darn it.

Note to self: always, always, always back everything up. Always!

I logged in to my bank account. Low. No one thousand four hundred dollars sitting there.

Would my time be better spent investigating the murder or reconstructing my records? I didn't even want to look at that box of receipts. I hated the business end, tallying figures, updating spreadsheets—that was a boring prospect. Figuring out the killer, wrapping up the case, and consequently getting the crime scene (and my thumb drive) released would be another way to come up with the records. Digging around for clues—that was an exciting possibility.

But, no…I ordered myself to work on the receipts for an hour, then promised myself I'd get busy searching for stalled vehicles that needed to be towed. First figure out where the money went, then make more money. I blew out a breath of air, blasting loose tendrils off my forehead, and began organizing the papers into small piles.

That is, until the doorbell rang. I slammed my laptop shut and jumped off my chair, all too eager for a distraction.

Chapter 4

Tanner walked through the door and dropped his head to his chest. I snaked my arms around his waist and gave him a squeeze, and the scent of Tanner flooded my senses. He ran his hands down my braid, causing electricity to buzz between us. Tanner and I used to go out, but I was with Ephraim now, so I took a deep breath and a step back.

"I talked to Ephraim."

"I know. He called me."

My heart clenched. Was I blushing yet again? "Why? Was it something I said?"

"No, he warned me not to involve you in this." Tanner let out a strained laugh. "But, look, here I am."

Glad that's all it was, I said, "I have news. I found out Clark was killed sometime Monday night. Her accounting partner found her the next morning. Do you have an alibi for that night?"

He shook his head. "I was by myself monitoring the no-parking zones."

"That's right, I knew that. Let's sit down." I led the way over to the couch. "Do you want something to drink?"

"No, thanks." He stretched his long legs out in front of him and leaned back into the sofa cushions.

I sat down and faced him, drawing my legs into my chest and wrapping my arms around my knees. "Did anyone see you? Did you tow anybody?"

"I hid my truck behind the brewery's dumpster. Probably no one saw me, but I could stop by the brewery and ask if anyone looked out the back door. The brewery is one of the few businesses not closed at night."

"No delivery trucks showed up?"

He bowed his head, looking tired and drawn. "No."

"No tows?"

"Not until about 8:30. The driver picked up his car right away, then I went home at nine."

I turned a hopeful gaze on my former boyfriend. "At least you have one witness, the one guy you towed. It's a start. You might have an alibi."

"Yeah." We both fell quiet. That tow took up only a small window of time. It would be nice to pinpoint the exact time of death.

"Did you know how she died?" I asked.

He pursed his lips and nodded. "Pushed down the stairs."

"How'd you hear about it? Was it in the news?" Ephraim had told me the sheriff's office was going to release that information.

"People were talking at the Chamber of Commerce meeting. Emery's firm did the accounting work for most of the businesses in town."

"Oh." Made sense. Spruce Ridge is a small town where everyone's acquainted with everybody else and news traveled fast. "No one knew the time of death?"

He made a small side-to-side motion with his head. "No." Then, he angled his body toward me and stroked my face with his hand.

A zing went through my stomach and I whispered, "Tanner…" He drew a line with his finger over my bottom lip. I jolted back and said, "Please, don't."

I would never cheat on Ephraim. Would I? *I don't know. Maybe. No!* But what can I say? I mean, come on, Tanner is totally *crushworthy.* And maybe I regretted our breakup a little bit.

He stood up. "Sorry, Laney, I shouldn't've done that." Tanner was a gentleman and respected my boundaries.

I stood, too, pretending that didn't just happen. "If I find out anything more, I'll call you."

"Okay."

"And let me know when the next Chamber meeting is. I'd like to be there. It wouldn't hurt to ask her other clients questions, am I right?"

"Good idea." Tanner headed for the door. "Thanks, Laney. I appreciate your help." He left, shutting the door behind him.

That was super awkward, but it gave me a little thrill to know Tanner still had feelings for me. The hot tow man had showed me how to operate my self-loader. He took me on ride-alongs, coached me in managing unhappy customers, and gave me a piece of his towaway business. He made learning how to haul cars fun. I liked Tanner's ease with the tow truck and how he handled people in general. You could count on Tanner. He was strong and powerful, like a double shot espresso, my favorite drink.

So now I wanted to slap myself. *Don't even think about it!* It might be a good idea to keep my distance from Tanner…but he needed my help. He seemed pretty depressed. Who wouldn't be? How could I not help him?

I could solve the crime, exonerate Tanner, and then I'd be able to get my accounting records back from the cops. Yup, that's what I needed to do, all right. Just help a friend. Get my records. Sure, let's go with that.

But first, I needed to make an effort to do some car hauling. I'd promised myself to try to get some paying work done.

The afternoon flew by as I cruised the highways for orange-tagged stalls. There weren't any. I stopped at the Homeowner's Association office at Ridgeside Condos to fulfill the contract I'd recently signed with them and make sure they didn't need any cars towed. There weren't any of those, either. Feeling disheartened and with not that much time left in the day, I spent a half-hour at the mall looking at shoes, then picked up Axle and headed home.

Procrastinate, much?

"Ephraim texted me that he's bringing dinner over," I told my roomie as we huffed up the stairs. Maybe I'd pick up some clues along with dinner.

Axle unlocked the door. "If that's an invitation, you're out of luck. I'm going out."

"Your loss."

I trudged back to my room to stare into my closet. Denim pencil skirt, blue stretchy tee shirt, blush-colored stacked heels. By the time I came back out, Axle had walked his dog and left, taking my Fiat with him. A teenaged boy without wheels of his own was tragic, yet I imagined he lived a full, rich teen life. He didn't talk much about what he got up to. Don't ask, don't tell.

The sound of cowboy boots on the stairs compelled me to the door and I welcomed Ephraim inside. I tried not to think about Tanner walking through that same door just a few hours before.

"My mom dropped off tamales at the station." The

sheriff set a brown bag with grease spots on the counter, and the smell of garlic, onion, cumin, and moist, warm corn husks filled the kitchen. He placed his cowboy hat on a hook by the door and ran a hand through his thick hair, ruffling up the ends. "I saved these aside, or there wouldn't have been any left."

"Nice!" I loved his mom's food just as much as the sheriffs at the station did. "You want a beer?"

"Sounds good, since I'm off tonight." He pulled me to him and kissed me in that slow, deep way, then said, "You look nice."

I flushed with pleasure. "Thanks. You do, too." The cowboy sheriff was out of uniform and looked even hotter in civvies if that was possible….blue jeans and a checked shirt with a white tee underneath.

Boss sniffed around Ephraim's legs, then the Rottweiler's cold nose poked my hand. "Good baby, good puppy," I said in my best puppy talk and gave him two treats from the bin, then pointed him toward his bowl full of kibble.

I turned on the oven to warm and extracted a cookie sheet from a low cabinet. Ephraim arranged the four super-sized tamales on the pan and I rummaged in the pantry for chips and salsa. I microwaved a bag of mixed southwestern vegetables and *walla!* dinner was ready. We took the hot food and our cold, long-neck bottles to the table and sat across from each other.

I glanced at the sheriff. "Everyone in town knows Emerald Clark fell down the stairs."

"If you checked the news release you would've found out all about it, too." His dimples came out.

I cracked a smile and teased, "Why should I do that when I have you?" But I got out my phone to look online.

"Don't bother." Ephraim patted my hand. "I told you everything in the release already."

I put down my phone. "What about the time of death? Is that public knowledge now?"

"Yes. Between 4:47 and 6:00 Monday night. The victim was on the phone, ending the conversation at 4:47, and the cleaning lady came on shift at 6. She checked the whole office, it was empty. She didn't check the stairway, though, so she didn't discover the body, but the victim was likely killed before the cleaning lady turned up."

That narrowed it down to a decently small window, but didn't hit the time frame of Tanner's alibi. "How do you know Clark didn't leave before the cleaning lady got there? Maybe she came back and was killed after she returned?"

"The cleaner saw the victim's car in the parking lot when she arrived, which was unusual, but she didn't let it concern her. Didn't even mention it until we questioned her about the vehicle. The car was never moved, we checked the parking lot surveillance tapes. Besides that, the victim had a self-defense class that night, and didn't show up for it. Everything confirms the window for the time of death, including the coroner's report." He bit off a big chunk of tamale and chewed.

"Self-defense class?"

He said around a full mouth, "Ironic, I know."

"And surveillance tapes. What luck." I flopped back in my chair. "Did the camera catch anyone coming or going?"

Once he swallowed, he said, "Unfortunately, no. The camera's not aimed at the door. It's aimed out toward the parking lot. Someone could've stowed their car around the corner and approached the building from the side."

I fiddled with my beer bottle. "All right. What about the cleaning lady? Could the cleaning lady have killed her?"

"There's no motive. They didn't know each other. She had no reason to even notice the victim's car, no reason to push her down the stairs. We're focusing our investigation elsewhere."

On Tanner? Tanner didn't have an alibi for that early in the evening. His one tow job was later that night.

Ephraim rose from his chair and wrapped up the last tamale neither of us could eat. We snuggled on the sofa to watch a romantic comedy. I couldn't help but compare the cowboy next to me with the tow man who had sat in this same spot earlier. Tanner hated rom-coms and preferred thrillers. Ephraim, however, was a romantic. The two are so different. Why am I attracted to both?

****

Will called me the next morning asking to meet, so I breezed down the highway to Denver in my little Fiat. Once I arrived, he ushered me into his office quick-like.

He got right to the heart of the matter. "I talked to the IRS, but they're only interested in working out a payment plan. If you don't remit the full amount at once, the IRS will charge interest and you might be subject to a late payment penalty."

Ugh. That's what I was afraid of.

I said, "Great." I was acting all grumpy and it wasn't Will's fault. "I don't expect you to handle this for free. You've done so much for me already." Will had helped me navigate through the estate documents when I inherited the tow truck and he'd registered my limited liability company for me. That involved moving my dad's LLC over to me. I can't explain the legal stuff, so it's a good thing to have Will on the family (zero) payment plan. I knew it was time to be a grownup and not expect free legal work anymore, but what can I say? I totally did. It was nice to have an attorney in the family.

"Delaney, it was only one phone call and you know I'm not going to charge you."

See what I mean?

Will added, "But let me loan you the money. It's not that much."

"It's a lot to me, but if you don't want to help me fight this, I'll figure it out myself." *As if!*

"It's not that I don't want to help, it just doesn't seem worth the effort." He rubbed his forehead. "Did you bring copies of your tax return? You probably filed a fairly simple form, I'm guessing? I'm not a tax attorney, but I can take a look at it."

"I didn't bring my return, sorry. I can email it to you, but I don't have the supporting documentation ready." I had to explain about Emerald Clark and my flash drive, glossing over the cause of death—all he needed to know was that she died suddenly and that the police had closed her office, sealing my records inside. Will responded with a grimace, but patiently listened to the end. As I expected, he didn't ask the cause of death. He wasn't curious that way.

He asked, "Do you want me to contact the police and try to get your thumb drive back?"

"No need. I've already asked Ephraim. I'm sure he'll get it to me as soon as he can." I sent my stepdad a smile. "Any day now."

"All right. Are you going to stop by and see your

mom before you leave town?"

"Did you tell her I was coming?" I focused on his face, very average looking, no distinguishing features. Even his brown, thinning hair was ordinary and his suit, clean and pressed, was last year's style.

"Yes."

"You told her about my tax problem?" My heart fell a couple thousand feet. Oh man, this was more painful than a $200 speeding ticket. I was more willing to take on the IRS than Mother.

She never believed I'd make a success of my dad's towing business. Now she'll be even more certain I was about to fail. She'd told me more than once I should use my social work degree and that I'm underemployed driving a tow truck. After graduating from college, I worked for Social Services for five years, but decided social work was not the career for me. I'd teared up at every dire situation, and those years were hard ones. My tender heart came into play with towing, too, but in a good way. It was gratifying to assist people stranded on the side of the road. I never really felt I was helping anyone as a social worker, at least not as much as I was helping people with car trouble.

My stepdad swept his hands up and down his face. "I don't keep anything from your mother."

I nodded in grim resignation. "I can't stop and see her today. I need to get back to Spruce Ridge. I have to monitor the towaway zones tonight." I had plenty of time. It was only an excuse get out of that conversation with Mother. I rose from my chair, but didn't head for the door quite yet. "Did I mention I got my commercial driver's license? Let Mom know, would you?" I couldn't help the dig. I was proud of passing the exam last month, but all the same I left Will's office with my grumpy mood intact. I needed my records organized. I needed to get right with the IRS. I needed to call Mom. It had been at least a week since I'd last talked to her, and I couldn't put her off too much longer.

I was such a crankypants on the drive back up the pass to Spruce Ridge that I could barely stand myself.

Chapter 5

At the Spruce Ridge exit, I spotted a stalled Nissan Rogue, front-wheel drive, orange-tagged by the city for removal. I pressed down on the Fiat's gas pedal and sped into town with the engine knocking, but when I returned with my tow truck the Nissan was gone from the side of the road. Some other tower had beat me to it.

I turned around for Spruce Ridge once again and rolled my truck to a stop at Ridgeside Condos. The Homeowner's Association had the authority to remove vehicles from the private lot, which was restricted to condominium owners only. I cruised up and down the rows, but all the windshields boasted parking permits. Fine by me. I didn't really like this part of the job.

Tanner's black truck was stopped in the entrance, so I pulled up alongside him and buzzed my window down.

"What are you doing here?" he asked. There were dark circles under his eyes.

"I got the contract with the condo association to monitor this lot." I gestured behind me.

"Sweet. I know Owen Eckerd had that contract last."

Owen Eckerd with the ugly green wrecker? My competitor who stole my last customer? The HOA took the contract away from him and gave it to me. *Yeah-ez!* That was almost as good as winning a trophy.

Tanner added, "Before Owen it was Mack and before him it was Hank."

"Hmmm. They change towing companies that much?" This didn't bode well for my tenure.

"I think they do." Tanner stared past my truck. "This is where Emery lived."

I swung my gaze over my shoulder and studied the first building, a gray structure with large windows and patio balconies. The second building matched, only it was white, and the third was pale yellow. The landscaping was well established and the whole complex looked nicely maintained. "Which building?"

"The gray one, second floor. You can see her balcony from here, the one with the white patio furniture." The balcony held pretty, white wicker chairs with orange and yellow cushions.

My gaze returned to Tanner. "How did you know she lived here?"

"I knew her for a long time." His face had a sad cast. Just how well had he known this woman? Not that I had any reason to wonder. He added, "She's done my books ever since I started in the business."

"You didn't know she was skimming when you recommended her to me, did you?" I stepped on the truck's parking brake and shoved the gearshift into park.

His eyes landed on mine. "Course not. I only just figured it out."

Our eyes locked, then I broke the connection and stared into my lap. "How did you come to use her? Did someone refer you to Emery?"

He gave me a thorough inspection and I squirmed. Did my questions sound like I was jealous? I tried to shut down that green-eyed monster.

He said, "Spruce Ridge Accounting represents a lot of towing companies. Emery understood the business."

A blast of air slapped my face through the open window and I was glad. Maybe my blushing hot cheeks would cool down. I told him, "I left a message for the other accountant, Megan Putnam, but she never called me back. I stopped by the accounting office yesterday and it was still closed."

"Yeah, I have a call in to Megan, too. I imagine she has a lot of calls to return." He tightened his jaw. "I spoke to the brewery owner and asked if anyone saw me Monday night. No one did."

"Ephraim told me Emery was killed between quarter to five and 6:00. I guess that news was in the papers."

"I was alone then. No alibi." He shut his eyes and pinched the bridge of his nose. "Okay, at least now I know what I'm dealing with."

I felt at a loss as to what more to say. "Are you all right, Tanner?"

His sudden smile made his face relax. He assured me, "I'm good. Laney, are you good?"

"Yeah." I heard tires crunch on the gravel behind me, and a pickup came into my rearview mirror. Since we were blocking the exit, I shifted my truck into drive and let off the brake. "Talk to you later."

I drove straight to the accounting office and climbed the first stairwell once more. The door was still locked, and when I knocked, no one answered. I left my business card stuck in the narrow space between the door and the frame with a note on the back to please call me.

I was sitting in my truck wondering what to do next when my phone rang on Del's Towing line. A man had locked his keys in his Honda Fit, front-wheel drive, in a parking lot near the intersection of Tall Chief Drive and Bald Eagle Way. It was rare for people to lock their keys in their cars since we all have keyless entry, but I had the tools to help them when they did. Five minutes later, I pulled my truck in next to the Honda. No one was waiting at the vehicle, so I looked around the parking lot, empty except for one other car nosed against an old building that had once been a gas station but now housed a wine tasting room. The garage doors were rolled up to give the place an open-air, European feel.

A man in his fifties, with short gray hair and thirty pounds of extra weight, stepped outside the wine-tasting room and strode up to me. "Where's Del?" He shoved his fists onto his hips. "Where's the tow truck driver?"

"That's me. I'm Delaney."

"I was expecting a man." His eyes drilled into me. "Are you going to be able to help me?"

Not another misogynist. Really? Again? I forced a smile. "Certainly. I have an unlock kit, and I'll have your vehicle open in no time." I hoped. Actually, I wasn't very proficient with the slim Jim.

"Humpf. We'll see." He wasn't even pretending to be polite. He propped a foot on the fender and leaned his elbow on his thigh, like he was going to sit back and watch the show. The jerk. My high-tech tow truck was more simple to use than the slim Jim. Unlocking a car door took some skill. I might be a girl who doesn't know a heck of a lot about motors and mechanical things (other than pressing that remote button), but push me and I rise to the challenge.

"Let me get my tools and I'll be right back." I managed to keep the anger out of my voice. I was the one the man spoke with on the phone. Did he think I was the office girl taking calls for the man who drove the truck? A slow boil simmered through my blood, but I told myself a job is a job and ran around to the back of my self-loader where the tools were stored in a compartment under the bed.

I extracted the case that held the flat, metal *thingie* with the little bend on the tip. Axle was really good at this and I'd watched him unlock car doors a dozen times. I slid the thin strap between the driver's window and the door frame and wiggled it around like I'd seen Axle do. When the lock popped up, I reached for the handle and opened the door.

Reeling in shock that I actually got the slim Jim to work, I almost fell off my silver, platform heels.

"There you go," I said in my most professional vehicle recovery agent voice. "How did you lock your keys inside anyway?" Of all the silly things I've done in the past, that wasn't one.

"I hit the power button on my way out of my Honda and locked my keys in the ignition." He pushed off the fender. With a smirk on his lips, he added, "I suppose you're going to charge me for this even though I didn't need a tow."

I clenched my fists but told him my fee in a polite voice. He paid with a credit card. I returned the tool kit to the truck and came back with one of my business cards with the logo of the black stiletto. "Please call me again if you ever need additional services. Here's my card."

He didn't take the card from my hand. "I'd never call a…uh, I won't need this done again. I'll be more careful in future."

My face burned and my throat constricted. "Thank you for using Del's Towing." I almost choked on those words.

He slid into his car, slammed the door shut, and off

he went. The chauvinist pig. Oink, oink. But I showed him. Snort!

The wine tasting room was calling me. Boy, I could use one of their samples. I knew the guy who ran the place, and alcohol was tempting right now, but if there was anything that could shove thoughts of bad customers aside it was thoughts of my flash drive at the accountant's office.

I drove back over there. The door was still locked. My card was still stuck in the crack. I left another phone message for Megan Putnam. Since I was getting nowhere with her, I returned to my truck and looped back around to Roasters on the Ridge—my pseudo office. If I could just pull my records together, I'd be done with the IRS headache, so I might as well keep working on that while waiting for the accountant to call. I hauled the box of paperwork down from my apartment to the coffee shop, and after I said hello to Kristen, I grabbed a table.

As soon as I'd popped open my laptop and brought out the first handful of receipts, DiNerdo entered the coffee shop. He was either waiting for me or had a sixth sense about me, because he always seemed to show up when I did. This was just that kind of a sucky day.

Even though I kept my head down and pretended to be invisible, he walked right up to my table. "Miss Morran."

I sucked on my lower lip. "Hello, DiNerdo."

"It's DiNardo."

No apologies this time. I'd called him that on purpose. My bad. I told him, "My attorney spoke with the IRS." That sounded more impressive than what it was.

He straightened his polka-dot bow tie in his nervous

55

way. "That doesn't preclude you from talking to me."

"It doesn't?" I tried to keep the snark out of my voice. "Are you getting a coffee?" The seductive aroma of the beans filled the coffee shop and I was about to get one for myself.

"Ah, yes, I probably should order something."

"Yes, you should, you're here often enough." I zigzagged through the tables over to the cash register with DiNerdo following on my heels. Guy, my favorite barista, took my order, a double espresso, and DiNerdo's, a hot English Breakfast tea with cream. I paid for both our drinks and stuffed a dollar in the tip jar. Yes, I couldn't pay for my taxes, but I could pay for my tax collector's coffee. I'm generous like that.

DiNerdo placed his hot tea on my table and took a seat. "Next drink's on me." Ugh, that meant there'd be another visit from him. Of course there would be. He asked, "When do you plan on settling the $1,437.12 you owe per tax code §2.3104.141a."

Pushy, pushy. I'm sure I had on a *oh-no-not-again* expression. "Can't you let up?" I leaned forward in my seat and propped my elbows on the table. "Cut me some slack, why don't ya?"

"No." His chair was across from me so we were facing each other.

"You have nothing better to do than hassle me? Am I your only case?"

"I have another appointment today, but you're first on my agenda."

"Yay, me." I bounced both hands off my chest and wondered who the other lucky person is. "Isn't there a chance the IRS is wrong? Can't you at least consider that possibility? I'm going to get my stuff together and I'll prove I don't owe anything." I gestured to the receipts next to my laptop and noticed several had fallen to the floor.

"The Internal Revenue never makes mistakes." He raised his right hand as if swearing on it. "You wouldn't try to evade paying your taxes? You won't hide from me, will you?"

"Hide from you? I would never." I totally would. My cheeks burned as I thought about it. "Well, I need to get everything ready for my attorney." I stared at my screen, hoping he would go away.

He stood up. "I'll be seeing you soon, Ms. Morran." Good. He was leaving.

"It's Delaney." I smiled even though I didn't feel like it. "See you later, DiNerdo."

"It's DiNardo."

"Oh, sorry. I keep forgetting." I'm not kidding, either. I did forget. I wasn't trying to press his buttons this time. *Yeesh.*

Note to self: Be nice.

After DiNardo made his exit—see what I did there? I got his name right—I spent the next hour going through invoices, then scanning them in Kristen's office, then entering numbers into a new spreadsheet, and finally totaling columns. I stuffed the receipts into file folders with labels and placed them back in the box. More than once I considered taking up Will's offer for a loan. How many extra tows would I need to pay him back? I sighed, thinking about the one lone roadside service today and the fact I hadn't hauled any cars the entire week before. Maybe what I needed to do was ask for repo work from the car dealership in town. Nancy Abington of Abington Motors had not called me to handle a repo in a very long time. Not my favorite work, but beggars can't be choosers. I'd take her a coffee and ask how's she's doing and then hit her up for a repo job.

I stuffed my box of files on the floor in Kristen's office, grabbed a caramel latte to-go for Nancy, and climbed into my self-loader. I connected with Pine Street, then headed south to the dealership near the mall. I alighted from the truck with Nancy's drink and asked for her at the reception desk.

Nancy came out from a door down the hallway. "Good afternoon, Delaney."

I beat it past the busy sales staff in their cubicles and handed Nancy her steaming latte. "Afternoon. This is for you."

"You're always so sweet to remember me."

"Of course." I took in Nancy's blonde-colored hair, her careful makeup, and her business suit. I was wearing my usual uniform of jeans and a stretchy top, but my silver platform heels were impressive if I could say so myself.

"Come on back." She led me into her office with the modern glass desk. The fragrance of her perfume lingered in the air.

"I'm here to bribe you for a repo assignment." I laughed and sat in her guest chair.

She went behind her desk to take her seat. "I don't have any for you right now."

I blew a sigh. "Oh well, thought I'd ask."

She fingered the necklace at her throat then fiddled with paperwork on her desk. Something was on her mind, so I waited. Finally, she asked, "You heard about Emerald Clark?" When I nodded, she went on. "It was all anyone could talk about at the Chamber meeting."

I really should start attending those Chamber meetings, but sitting right in front of me, here and now, was a great opportunity. "What are they saying?"

"Just how awful it was, a young woman dying like that. Sad, you know?" She gave me an intense look. "Are you investigating?" *Ah-ha*. This was what Nancy wanted to talk about. She knew better than most that I'd caught a murderer, or more truthfully, I'd barely escaped being killed by a murderer, in a prior homicide investigation.

"Sort of." I asked her, "Who do you think killed her?"

"Well," she said as she scooted her chair in closer, "the police questioned me. I think they suspect me."

My eyebrows shot up. "Why you?"

"Emerald Clark was the accountant for the car dealership. And I'm not the only client of hers questioned by the police. We all waited at the sheriff's station together. I know who the other suspects are." Her voice was giddy with knowledge.

I gulped. "You do?"

She had on a *you-heard-me-right* look. "I have a list of suspects for you."

Yeah-ez! I'm down with that. I reached in my purse for the small spiral and pen I kept in the pocket. I posed pen over paper. "Tell me."

"Tanner Utley. He's a tow truck driver like you."

"I know him." This was disappointing. I was hoping for fresh blood.

"Okay. Do you know Mike Horn with Main Street Coffee? And there's Noel Yarborough at the winery. And Megan Putnam, the other accountant. They were at the sheriff's station, too." Her eyes dilated in excitement.

I knew Mike Horn and Noel Yarborough. They

weren't exactly friends of mine, but we were all business owners in this small town where everyone knows everybody else. "I figured Putman would be questioned. I've left her several messages but she hasn't called me back. Did you see anyone else?"

"Anne Sullivan. She owns the flower shop by the mall. That's it." Nancy sat back in her chair and folded her arms over her chest. "I mean, there may have been more, but those were the ones I saw."

"Okay." I finished writing the last name. Four suspects not counting Tanner and Nancy—Mike Horn, Noel Yarborough, Anne Sullivan, and Megan Putnam—assuming the business partner was also a suspect. Tanner didn't do it, and it should be easy to eliminate Nancy from the suspect list, too. "Do you have an alibi, Nancy? Clark died between a quarter to five and six on Monday night." I felt a pinch of guilt for asking.

Amusement lit Nancy's eyes. "I was here at the dealership. My sales staff can vouch for me."

"That's good." I laughed nervously, but scribbled that down, then shoved my notebook into my purse. Nancy seemed captivated by the crime, but was a very unlikely suspect herself, especially now that she was cleared by an alibi. My mind was already mulling over the other possibilities and who had a motive. While I'd crossed paths with Mike Horn and Noel Yarborough many times, I didn't know Anne Sullivan at all. I didn't know Megan Putnam, either. Those were the two unknowns, Anne and Megan, more suspicious than the others in my opinion. I felt comfortable enough questioning Mike and Noel, and would speak with them soon to eliminate them properly. Anne and Megan might prove trickier to question.

Nancy tapped her temple with one finger. "I can tell you're thinking. What is it?"

"I was thinking about motives. Do you have any idea why Clark's clients would want to kill her?" I studied Nancy's face. Did she know about the skimming? How many people knew? Tanner believed he was the only one to discover Clark's crime, and I didn't want to tell Nancy that Tanner was the top suspect, or at least he thought so.

"No, not really." Nancy crossed her legs and jiggled her foot. "But there must be a reason for the police to question her clients," she added in a low voice. "So, the killer had something to do with her work."

"Yes." For a long moment we were both silent.

"I'm a little worried about that," she added.

"You are?" I waited for her to bring it up, but she didn't mention the embezzlement. I leaned an elbow on her desk. "I'm worried, too, and it's not just about this murder. I've got a lot on my plate right now. Maybe you could give me some advice." Nancy was at the helm of a profitable commercial enterprise and would have insightful information.

She sat forward. "What? What's the matter?"

It all came tumbling out. All my problems. The taxes. The flash drive. I said, "I need to get inside that accountant's office. It's going to take me way too long to recreate the records and there's this nerdy tax collector after me. He's like a persistent dog with a bone."

She tapped her desktop with fingers loaded with diamonds. "Be insistent with the police. Tell them you need your thumb drive and don't take no for an answer. Be assertive. Don't stand down." This self-assured business woman would take that attitude.

Being firm wasn't going to work for me, but I didn't argue. Nancy was only trying to help. I just needed to trust that Ephraim would come through, although he always went by the book, so who knew how long it would take for me to get that flash drive.

Nancy asked, "Anything else on your mind?" I gave her a questioning look. "You were going to write Rob at the prison. I was wondering if you'd written to him."

Rob Abington was Nancy's ex-husband and the former owner of the dealership. She'd taken over the business when he was sent to prison. She'd known I'd once thought Rob might have information about my dad's hit-and-run accident. "Not yet. Have you heard from him?"

"No." Nancy gave me a grimace and an eye roll.

The receptionist poked her head in the door. "Your next appointment is here, Nancy."

"I'll be going then." I rose from my chair. We said our goodbyes and I started down the narrow hall past the sales staff's work stations. I almost knocked into Owen Eckerd marching toward Nancy's office. He angled his body sideways to avoid me, and I did the same to avoid him, then he kept going without a word of acknowledgement.

That made me wonder if Nancy was giving Owen the repo work. That's probably what she was doing and didn't want to tell me. Why would she give Owen the assignments? Because he's a man and the work is dangerous? Would Nancy do that to me?

I could deal with repos. I wasn't afraid. I was tough. But even as I thought it, my voice within scoffed at this.

Repos were risky…but necessary. Tow truck drivers recovered cars all the time from people in default on their loans. And who am I if not a tow truck driver? This is who I am now. Capturing vehicles from owners who didn't make their payments.

Maybe that was how Benedict DiNardo felt about tax collection. Was I no better than the taxman?

Chapter 6

"Kristen, I'm here. You have time for a break?" I asked as soon as I walked through the door of Roasters on the Ridge, my nose twitching at the smell of the coffee.

"Sure." Her grin took up her whole face. "And no worries. He's not here." Before I returned, I'd first texted Kris to make sure DiNerdo wasn't lurking around the coffee shop.

She unwound the café apron from her waist and stuffed it under the counter, then handed me an espresso in a tiny cup. And yes, it was adding up to be a two-espresso day. We parked ourselves at our favorite table in the window and I slurped down a mouthful like the caffeine addict I am.

I set down my cup. "I think I've had just about enough of DiNerdo. He's driving me crazy."

She said, "Is that all that's bothering you?"

"Well, there is something else. I'm not sure I want to do repo work." I tossed my red plait over my shoulder. If Owen Eckerd was doing the work, did I want it? I was better than that dickhead. And besides, even though I asked Nancy for an assignment, repos made my stomach hurt. "Repossessing cars feels mean, Kris. It seems like a moral gray area to me."

She raised her hands in the universal sign of surrender. "So, we're having this talk again. Weren't you just at Abington's trying to get a repo?"

I bobbed my shoulders up and down in a stretch. "I know, I know. I was," I said in a sing-song voice. "And yes, buyers who don't make their payments are supposed to return their cars voluntarily. They shouldn't keep them, otherwise it's stealing. So I'm in the right, they're in the wrong."

Kristen nodded in agreement. "That's correct. Don't forget it."

I sank back into the chair. "But repos are no fun. No fun at all."

She patted my hand. "Work isn't always fun. There are a lot of things you like, remember that. Being your own boss. Not sitting at a desk all day. Working outside." She gave me another upbeat smile. "Helping people."

I had to admit all that was true. "Well, I guess I don't really need to worry about it yet. It's not as if Nancy gave me a job." I tried not to think about Owen getting the work. "Hey, I've got something to tell you. Nancy was taken in for questioning."

Her hand slid over her mouth. "Really?"

"And she saw Tanner, Mike Horn, Noel Yarborough, and Anne Sullivan at the station." I checked the names off my fingers. "Those are some of Clark's clients. They brought in Clark's business partner, Megan Putnam, too."

Her eyebrows elevated in a question. "Who was that last client?"

"Anne Sullivan. She runs the flower shop over by the mall."

"I know Anne from church."

I rubbed my hands together. "You can introduce us. What's she like?"

"She seems nice, I guess. You could come to church with me."

"Sure," I agreed. Sweet Kristen never pressured me.

"So, Tanner's a suspect, huh?" she asked.

"He is. In fact, he's worried the sheriff's focused on him." A part of me scrunched up inside, anxious on his behalf.

She crinkled her nose. "Why?"

"Please keep this between the two of us. He thinks Clark was skimming from his account and the police believe he killed her over it. You and I both know that's all wrong, Tanner would never hurt anyone." The police have to realize this. What did they know...what clues had they uncovered that pointed to him?

Kristen said, looking a bit shocked, "Skimming! Boy, am I glad I use an accounting firm from Denver, a firm my dad uses."

I took a bracing sip of my espresso. "I hear ya. I'm planning to talk to Mike and Noel and find out if they have alibis."

She held up a finger like *hold on a sec*. "Why do you need to investigate this time?"

I placed my hand across my chest. "You know why. Tanner's a suspect. Plus, if the case is solved, I can get my flash drive back." I wouldn't need to go through any more of the receipts I'd left in Kris's office. I'd hardly made a dent.

"Right."

"Pretty big incentive."

"There's that, except..." Her expression showed deep-seated concern. "You'll avoid repos, but not a murder investigation? Which is more dangerous?"

She had a point.

The coffee shop door banged open and shut as Byron and Axle stepped into the center of the room. "Hey, you two." Kristen waved them over. "Are you in need of coffees?"

Byron said, "Not me. I'm just droppin' Axle off."

"Did you close shop early?" I asked him.

"Nah, Shannon's holdin' down the fort." Shannon was Byron's niece who worked part time for him. She was also Axle's main squeeze. Byron announced, "Axle's goin' to look at a used Nissan Altima."

I turned to Axle. "You're going to buy a car?" I was the one who usually ferried Axle around town. It would be weird not to be needed anymore.

"I'm just looking at it, I'm not going to buy if it needs too much work." Axle slouched against the wall. I recognized his *trying-to-act-cool* look.

"Watchu all talkin' about when we came in?" Byron pulled out a chair with a loud scrape.

"Suspects in the Emerald Clark murder investigation, all accounting clients of hers." I listed them again, "Mike Horn, Noel Yarborough, Anne Sullivan." I left off Tanner. "And her business partner, Megan Putnam."

"I'm thankful I didn't use Spruce Ridge Accounting or I'd be on that list, too," Kristen put in.

"I use Putnam and nobody's contacted me." Byron looked slightly doubtful.

"Well, I'm getting a coffee before my buddy gets here." Axle crossed the distance to the counter and we all stared after him. He didn't seem too interested in the murder.

Kristen nudged my elbow and mouthed the words, "Axle's getting his own car?"

I nodded at my friend, then asked Byron, "You know Anne Sullivan?"

"Can't say I do."

I was disappointed, but at least Kristen knew her. "Byron, will you go with me to the wine tasting room to talk to Noel Yarborough? Kris, here, doesn't drink," I pointed to my friend, "Axle's too young to drink, although he doesn't think so, and I can't ask Ephraim."

"You know I don't drink either." Byron is a recovering alcoholic and an ex-con who was given a job and a second chance by my dad. He'd done all right for himself, now that he owned my dad's old autobody shop, and I cared a great deal about Byron's opinion. He had wisdom beyond mine and was sort of like my surrogate dad. He'd gone with me into dangerous situations before. He asked me, "Why you want to question anybody, anyways?"

I shrugged. "You know me."

Axle returned to the table and stood on the other side of Kristen's chair, drumming his fingers on the side of his to-go cup. Kris looked up at him. "A Nissan Altima, huh?"

"Yeah, I think the Altima is bitchin'."

Byron suggested, "Why don't you ask Tanner ta' go with ya', Delaney?"

I said, "I guess that would work. Or I could try catching up with folks at the next Chamber meeting. Noel and Mike are members." Or, heck, I could go by myself to question them, no biggie. It wouldn't really be dangerous.

The old man's knees snapped as he stood. "See you later, Delaney, Kristen. Good luck, Axle."

I sprang to my feet and hitched my bag onto my

shoulder. "Yeah, ditto that. I'm heading out, too."

Byron banged through the door and I trooped out after him. Axle came behind us with his latte gripped in one fist. Ax and I watched Byron take off in his white Ford 150, an all-terrain 4-wheel-drive, then I buddy-punched my lil' cuz' in the arm.

I asked, "So, I'm not going to be your taxi anymore?"

"What? Why do you say that?"

"Keep up, here. You're buying a car." I gave him an eyeroll.

Axle gave my arm a sharp pinch. "You're going to miss having me around."

"Of course not. Why would you think that?" But the smug little twerp wasn't wrong. "Come here." I opened my arms wide, but it was obvious he didn't want the bear hug, so I let my arms drop. I swatted him instead. "Looks like your friend's here."

A Volkswagen Jetta, front-wheel drive, careened into the lot, and Axle jogged the few steps over. He ripped open the passenger door and jumped in. When the Jetta's tires crunched out of the lot and down Pine Street, I slogged across the pavement to my red tow truck. I fired her up and arrived back at Spruce Ridge Accounting in five minutes.

I took the front stairs two at a time and tried the door. Again.

Surprise.

It was unlocked.

The miniscule waiting room had industrial gray carpet, a bubbling aquarium, and two blue padded chairs with metal legs. A closed interior door bisected the opposite wall. The air smelled of dust and carpet. An itsy-bitsy camera in the corner of the ceiling pointed toward the entrance.

"Hello? Anyone here?" I asked the empty room.

All was quiet, in the way of unoccupied spaces, until I heard footsteps on the other side of the door. I'd been down that hallway before when I'd met with Clark. Someone must be working today.

"Hello?" I called again. I don't know why, but I was as nervous as a fluttering aspen.

The door pushed open and a woman stepped through. My first thought was that she was plain. About my age with thin brown hair hanging past her shoulders. She had a long nose and square chin. But her cerulean blue eyes nudged her from plain toward pretty.

"Can I help you?" she asked.

I gave her an uncertain smile. "Yes, at least I hope you can. Are you Megan Putnam?"

"I am."

"My name's Delaney Morran. I left you a message." That didn't seem to register with her. "Emerald Clark was my accountant." One of her eyebrows kicked up higher than the other. "I'm sorry for your loss," I said, a bit late. "What happened to your business partner must have hit you hard."

"Yes, it did."

"I need some accounting work done. Do you have a minute to talk?"

She hesitated for a couple of seconds, then said, "Come on back." She pivoted on her low heels, and I followed her along the hallway, anxiety giving way to relief. We passed Clark's office, but the door was shut. We entered the next office down, and the accountant eased herself into a chair behind the desk.

I helped myself to the visitor's chair. "I own Del's Towing. I left a thumb drive with Emerald Clark and I need that drive back. It has my business records on it and I have a tax deadline I'm trying to meet."

"I'm sorry, but the police cleared out her office files and they haven't returned anything yet."

I slumped back in my seat. "Can you take a look? Maybe it's in the bottom of a drawer or something."

She dismissed my request with a wave of her hand. "It wouldn't be. Emery wouldn't have tossed it in a drawer. I'm sure the flash drive is secured with your file."

I asked, "Will you please check anyway?"

"I'm telling you the police have everything, Delaney." Her blue eyes were riveting, her best feature. She oozed self-confidence, sitting tall with square shoulders and a good posture. And she wasn't going to help me with my thumb drive.

My gaze circled around the top of the ceiling then returned to her. "Do you know anyone who would want to harm Emery?"

"No." She looked at me directly. "Why are you asking me this?"

"How about unhappy clients? Anyone complain?"

Her eyes flicked to the left. "I don't know. None of *my* clients ever complained, that's for sure. Why?"

"It's just me hoping the police solve the case soon so I can get my flash drive back." The police had probably already interrogated her thoroughly about Clark's clients, but what if they were looking in the wrong direction? And me, too? What if we should be searching for a boyfriend? There was more than one type of motive to consider. I said, "Did Emery have a boyfriend?"

Megan's forehead wrinkled and her lips twitched down. "I can't talk about my former business partner."

I rocked back in my seat. "Really?"

She shook her head side to side. "I'm sorry I can't help you with your records, either. Is there anything else?"

I thought I might as well ask, "Can you tell me who Emery's clients were?" There were probably plenty more than the ones Nancy Abington spotted at the sheriff's office.

Megan flipped her brown hair back. "No, that's against client confidentiality."

Even though Megan was going to stay tight-lipped and probably just wanted me to leave, I took a steely breath and pushed forward. "I heard a rumor that she was skimming her client's accounts." I crossed my fingers behind my back hoping Tanner wouldn't mind me sharing this, but undoubtably the sheriff had questioned her about his suspicions already.

Megan jolted upright as if she'd been struck by a cattle prod, then she regained control and folded her hands on her desk. "You can't believe everything you hear."

"Sorry." I could tell a flush started at my neckline. I couldn't help but feel guilty, like a nasty gossip. "You're right. I shouldn't repeat rumors." Tanner had warned me that he might be wrong. "I'm still going to need an accountant. Will you have time to look at my records once I get the flash drive back? The IRS says I owe them taxes, but I don't think I do. Can you help with that?"

She stood up. "Call me and we'll schedule an appointment. I'm pretty busy, but I'll make the time."

I breathed a sigh of relief. "Here's my card. I left one in your door, but here's another one." I fished around in my bag for my business cards and drew one out. I placed it on her desk, glad this accountant was willing to squeeze me in.

Megan walked me down the hall and through the connecting door to the waiting room. A man sat in one of the padded blue chairs. His suit was stylish, but crumpled, like he'd had a long day at work, and his tie was loosened at his throat. His precision hair style included a little wave above his forehead. Brown hair, brown eyes, close shave. A fellow accountant? A lawyer? One of the two.

"I'll be right with you, Grayson." Megan pointed her chin toward the exit. "Delaney, call my office to make that appointment."

"I will. Thanks." I stole another glance at the man before the door closed behind me.

Running late now, I sped my truck over to Main Street to stake out the alley behind the loading docks. I was still wearing my silver platform heels because I hadn't had time to change into my yellow work boots. Oh well, I'd show some style to any soreheads who got their cars towed tonight.

Before my shift was over, I hauled two illegally parked vehicles, a Toyota Camry, front-wheel drive, and a Subaru Forester, all-wheel drive. The drivers didn't thank me, but my bank account did. I had enough to pay my electric and phone bills. Sorry, Mr. DiNerdo, but those came first. I needed my phone to do my work, and Axle wouldn't appreciate the electricity getting cut off. Besides, these two tows didn't add up to enough to pay the whole tax bill. If I got more than a few tows the tax bill would be next, I promised myself. That is, if I decided not to fight the IRS.

I had one last surveillance pass to do between the old brick buildings and the graffitied loading docks before calling it a night. My window was down and the cool night air caressed my face, keeping me alert. Just a half hour to go. A diesel sounded in the distance, then Ephraim's white four-door Chevy Silverado pickup with *Sheriff - Clear Creek County* painted black on white turned in the alley.

We simultaneously got out of our vehicles and met at the back of the tow truck. The alley was dark, but we stood under a security motion light, and pinpoints of stars burned overhead.

"Hey handsome." I rubbed my hands up and down my arms, chilled from the night air.

He slipped his jacket around my shoulders, grabbed both sides of the collar, and pulled me in for a kiss. The kiss knocked me breathless and made my heart jump like a truck engine on high octane. A flash of heat shot through my entire body, and I may have let out a big sigh.

He said, "I've missed you."

"I've missed you, too. I guess we've both been pretty busy."

"What's keeping you so occupied?"

My gaze zinged around the alley. "Towaway zones. Blocked loading docks. You know I do this every Tuesday and Thursday."

"That's all you've been doing?" His eyes twinkled and his dimples came out. If he suspected me of investigating he would be right. But I wasn't investigating at the moment.

"Ah, yeah, I'm busy towing. Doing some car

hauling." Monitoring the no-parking zones was all I'd been doing for the last four hours, anyway. Not to toot my own horn, but I could be sharp on my feet with evasive answers like that when I had to be. *Heh, heh.* "Anything new with the murder investigation?"

"I knew it! I knew you'd bring it up. Have you been asking questions, Delaney?"

Busted. What can I say to that? I answered, "No comment."

"Delaney, what have you been doing?" He gave me a *fess-up or else* look.

"I did ask Megan Putnam if she could look for my thumb drive," I admitted. "Ephraim, I really need it back. Putnam wouldn't even look for it. Can't you help me?"

"To be fair to Putnam, Clark's files were taken into evidence and her office locked up. No one is supposed to go in there."

I felt a sharp pang of disappointment. "What about you? Can't you go in? I need that thumb drive." I heard my voice rise and swallowed hard. I pictured DiNerdo waiting at the coffee shop bright and early tomorrow morning. I planned to avoid him and was not looking forward to abandoning my morning caffeine ritual.

He said, "The FDA specialist from the Denver Crime Lab still has the evidence boxes. Sorry."

"What's the FDA? I thought that meant Food and Drugs."

"Forensic Data Analysis. They focus on financial records." His hand caressed the back of my neck. "You'll be the first person I call when they're done."

At least the investigators were looking into Clark's business practices. If she was embezzling, they would likely identify her other victims and add even more names to their suspect list. More names than Tanner's. I said, "There's a surveillance camera in the accounting office reception area."

"Good job noticing that. You're smart and observant, Delaney. The camera is small and not many people would spot it. The perpetrator must have avoided it, though, because the camera did not record any images of visitors that night."

I was silent for a few moments, then asked, "You're sure the camera in the parking lot didn't capture anything either, right?"

"The camera recorded movement, but nothing that can identify the killer." A crease formed on his forehead. "You're asking the right questions, Delaney, and I'll admit we aren't getting very far yet, but it'll help when the forensic results come back. Please don't stir the pot. I don't want anything to happen to you. And I'll look out for your thumb drive, I promise. If I can get it for you, I will."

"Thanks." I rubbed his arm. "Is there anything I can do for you?"

His eyes strayed to my silver platform heels and back up to my red cheeks. "I wish, but not tonight. I need to get back to the station." He leaned in for another kiss and I snuggled closer to him. After his lips released mine, I slid out of his jacket and handed it to him, then he got in his truck and left.

I might as well write off that thumb drive as a loss.

Chapter 7

I spent the next morning at Roasters on the Ridge with my laptop, organizing the last of my receipts. I hated doing the books, but didn't mind sitting in the window of the coffee shop. That's where I'd parked myself. I'd decided I wasn't going to let DiNerdo keep me from coming to my favorite venue. Working at Roasters was like getting a coffee-scented embrace, as long as DiNerdo didn't show up and push me out of here.

Almost done, I took my eyes off the stack of papers and plucked up my espresso. The place was nearly deserted. Two teens drank lattes at one table and a young mom rocked a baby stroller at another. The rest of the tables were empty, and Guy, the barista, was cleaning the coffee machines.

Tanner swung through the front door and his long legs carried him across the room to me. "Are you busy?"

"Just finishing up." I saved my spreadsheet, exited the program, and shut my laptop.

"There's a Chamber event today. I wasn't going to go, but the reminder popped up on my phone and I thought, why not? You want to go with me?"

"Yes, I certainly do." I swallowed the last of my coffee and gathered up my stuff. Tanner shepherded me outside, and I was glad I was wearing my business appropriate, black high heels.

I stopped at Tanner's truck to ask, "I hope it's all

right to talk about the skimming. I told Kristen and Axle knows. I asked Megan about it, but told her it was a rumor. I didn't mention you or anything."

He nodded. "I suppose you need to bring it up, but I'd appreciate you keeping my name out of it."

I answered, "I can do that."

"What did Megan say when you talked to her?"

"She said not to believe rumors." I noticed his frown. "But what could she say? She couldn't really admit knowing about it. But I'm not giving up, don't worry about that, Tanner."

"Okay. See you in a few minutes at the meeting." He swung in to his cab and drove out of the lot while I crossed the distance to my truck.

The Chamber of Commerce met in a warehouse-type office building on Industrial Lane. Inside the prefab structure, the metal ceiling towered twenty feet above our heads and the hard cement floor covered the ground under our feet. Metal folding chairs were arranged in a semi-circle, and a long table against the far wall held store-bought cookies and giant urns of weak coffee. The setting reminded me of what I assumed an AA meeting would look like.

I scanned the small crowd for suspects when my eyes alighted on that nice Nancy Abington talking to that awful Owen Eckerd. Is the auto dealer giving Owen with the ugly green tow truck a repo assignment? Is he telling her what a poor tow truck driver I am? That customers didn't want me to tow their cars and preferred him? I ambled along the cookie table to weasel my way in closer, but I couldn't hear their words among the loud conversations echoing in the high-ceilinged room. Someone reaching for a coffee cup brushed my arm, and

I took a step back, bumping the table and knocking over a stack of napkins. Still talking to Nancy, Owen threw a glance in my direction, then turned his back to me.

I was restacking the napkins and grumbling to myself about Nancy and Owen when Tanner grasped my elbow.

"There you are." He led me to the chairs and we sat down next to each other.

Everyone took seats in front of the wooden podium, while a committee chairmen began to make announcements about city construction projects, street improvements, and economic development. After his talk there was a chance to mingle and exchange business cards. Recognizable business owners from the upscale boutiques on Main Street headed to the refreshment table. The swell of conversation grew and the decibel level in the room rose higher. This was not only a chance to dig up murder clues, this was a chance to network, and I should take advantage of the opportunity.

I was about to cross the room when Hailey with Friendly Finance appeared at Tanner's side. A few years older than me, she wore a professional gray business suit and starched white blouse. Her short charcoal hair showcased her high cheekbones, lovely, long eyelashes, and flawless mahogany skin. She said, "Hello, you two."

"Hey lady." Tanner gave her a brief side-hug. Hailey was the finance office's manager, loan officer, and repo agent, all in one, and she gave her repo assignments to Tanner. I appreciated Hailey and often asked her for business advice like I did Nancy.

"I suppose you heard about Emerald Clark?" I laughed with a nervous quaver.

"Who hasn't?" Hailey flicked her gaze toward me

and her pretty eyes tilted up at the corners.

"Was she your accountant, too? She seemed to work for everyone around here."

"No. I do my own books."

"Do you know anything about what happened to her?"

Hailey ripped her gaze from me to focus on Tanner. "I did hear that Emery broke up with her boyfriend and he wasn't too happy about it."

I glanced at Tanner and found a scowl on his face. I asked Hailey, "Who was her boyfriend?"

Hailey and Tanner exchanged a look I couldn't read, then Hailey said, "I need to talk to the Chamber president. See you later." She walked away with purposeful steps.

"Who was her boyfriend?" I asked Tanner.

He shrugged a *who-knows* gesture. "I'm going to mingle. You should, too." He strode off in another direction.

The business owners all looked deep in conversation, their words loud and indistinguishable in that way of large gatherings, and I was shy about talking to strangers. I looked around for anyone I knew from my suspect list, but the owner of Main Street Coffee—Mike Horn—was not in attendance today. Neither was the winery owner—Noel Yarborough. So much for questioning either of them. I didn't know what the flower shop lady looked like—Anne Sullivan—so I asked the woman refilling the cookie plates if she knew Anne. She pointed to a woman over by the coffee urn.

Anne must be older than me by twenty-plus years, in her size XL tee shirt, stamped with a hummingbird among purple flowers. Her lavender pants matched, and her straw, flower-embossed handbag hung from an elbow.

I started that way, but Nancy stopped me and asked jokingly why I didn't bring lattes seeing as the coffee's so bad, then the owner of the downtown art gallery stopped me since I monitor his towaway zones, then the president of the Chamber stopped me because he wanted to know why I wasn't a member yet. All that made me feel good. It was nice to be recognized and part of the community. So, after I spent a polite couple of minutes with each of them—getting in some networking after all—I hightailed it to the coffee table but Anne Sullivan was no longer there.

Frustrated, much?

Spotting her going out the exit, I sprinted through the door after her.

I cried out, "Anne Sullivan?" She stopped and spun around, and I stumble-halted up to her. "Anne?"

"Yes, that's me."

"I'm Delaney Morran." I stuck out my hand and she shook it. "Do you have a minute to talk to me? I wanted to ask you about Emerald Clark."

Anne retracted her hand to run her fingers through her short, pixie-cut hair. "Why would you want to talk to *me* about *her*?"

"She was your accountant, right?"

"Yes."

"I'm trying to get information about her."

"Why? Are you with the police?"

"No." I considered the woman in front of me. She appeared the sturdy type, capable of pushing someone down the stairs in spite of her grandmotherly appearance.

"Then, I'm not sure I should speak to you." Anne

cast her eyes down. "I don't like to speak ill of the dead."

"So, you know something? Something…ill, I mean bad, about Clark?" I tried not to sound too eager.

The older woman blasted me with a cold look. Like the temperature dropped to below freezing. "I'm sorry, but I can't talk about it." She hustled to her car, moving at a speed faster than I believed possible for her size. She shoehorned herself into a Dodge Dart, front-wheel drive, and pulled out of the lot. A *Save the Sperm Whale* sticker covered her back bumper.

Disappointing, much?

Anne knew something, and I might need to enlist Kristen's help the next time I tried talking to her.

I went back inside and found Tanner. He was ready to leave, so we both took off. I stopped at the supermarket to fill up a shopping cart. Cereal for Axle. Kibble for Boss. Hard boiled eggs for me. Chips, popcorn, donuts, and other crap for all of us.

My phone rang with a call from Patrick Crump and I answered it, even though I was standing in the checkout line. Crump worked for Nancy Abington at Abington Auto Store, and some calls you just have to take. This could be work.

"Patrick, do you have a repo for me?"

"Yes. Nancy told me you stopped by the dealership, and since this new repo just popped up on our radar, she asked me to call you." Crump was an all-business, hard-ass type. When we first worked together we butted heads, but I'd learned to appreciate his toughness. You had to be tough in the repo business.

"Oh, I'm glad you called." But I had to wonder, did Nancy feel guilty for giving Owen all her repo work, so she decided to throw me an assignment to keep me happy? Or maybe Nancy wasn't giving Owen the repos. Maybe he'd been at her office asking for work, same as me. And he could've been sucking up to Nancy at the Chamber of Commerce meeting, too.

Crump said, "It's a Hyundai Elantra, and I found it in the workout center parking lot." He gave me the owner's name and read off the numbers in the VIN and the license plate.

"On my way now." I quickly paid for the groceries and ran out the door, clutching my bags. It was mid-morning and the day was perfect. Blue sky, white clouds, high seventies. I jumped on the freeway, my truck sailing up the hill and breezing down the other side, then I got off at the next exit. The fitness center was only a few blocks off the interstate, and I was there in minutes.

A shady tree almost hid the Elantra at the edge of the parking lot. The driver had pulled his vehicle through the row of parked cars, either that or he'd backed in, so nothing was blocking his front end. Lucky for me since the Elantra is front-wheel drive.

When I slid down from the cab my black heels hit the ground. I scurried over to verify the VIN through the windshield. Once back in my truck, I pressed the button on the wireless controls. With a whine of hydraulics, the T-shaped bar lowered to the ground, the crossbar extended, and the claws rotated around the front tires. Another swish and hiss, and the boom raised the target vehicle off the ground. The operation took less than thirty seconds.

A man bounded out the door to the workout center, a phone in one hand and car keys in the other. I pulled onto the street and he threw his phone after me. The phone hit the pavement and shattered. I stopped the truck and rubbed my temples, staring in the mirror. The man was pacing in a circle, flinging his arms around, and before I could talk myself out of it, I angled up to the curb, shut off the engine, and walked back.

I said, "Sorry, but this is my job."

He swatted the air. "Yeah, yeah." His left front tooth had a little chip in it, giving him a child-like appearance. He was wearing sweatpants and a tee shirt, but didn't appear to be the usual muscle-bound, beefy guy who pumped iron. His arms were thin and his chest non-existent. He must've just joined the gym recently. His light brown hair was thinning and it looked like he was trying to grow a beard, but was underperforming there too.

"Can I help you find your phone?" My gaze searched the ground at our feet.

Bits of metal and glass littered the spot where the phone impacted the pavement, and the two of us scrambled around to pick up the pieces, but it was broken to smithereens. He opened his palm and I deposited some fragments into his hand.

He said, "Thanks."

"You're Clyde Dankworth?" I checked his name in my notes. When he nodded, I asked, "You need a ride?" The guy was stranded without a car or a phone.

"Yeah." He rubbed the peach fuzz on his chin. "Are you taking my car to the dealership?"

"That's where I'm headed."

"Can you take me there, too? I'd like to make arrangements to get caught up on my payments."

His anger had seemed to evaporate when he took it out on his phone, and he was being reasonable now. He'd bring his loan current and get his Elantra back. The guy was going to be all right, so I cheered up a little.

"That sounds like a good idea," I told him.

I retraced my steps back to the self-loader and opened the passenger door. He joined me, and after I moved the grocery bags to the back, he hoisted himself in.

At the dealership, I deposited his Elantra behind the oil change area and texted Patrick Crump. Clyde said thanks and headed toward the entry door. The dealership sent out recovery checks at the end of the month, so I had that to look forward to. Then I could pay the IRS. Or not. I was still planning to dispute the amount regardless of the seven day deadline DiNardo had given me.

When I was chugging down Main Street ten minutes later, Crump called and I hit the button for speaker phone. He asked, "Where did you leave the Elantra?"

"Behind the oil change service entrance."

"Where?"

"The place you told me to leave the cars."

"It's not there."

"Whaaat?" I turned right on a side street and stopped at the curb.

"I guess I should've had you haul it inside. The owner probably came by and snatched it back."

"No!" I blushed and my nose turned red.

"Sure. It's happened to us before. This isn't the first time."

"Gee, that's terrible. So, you'll call me when you locate the vehicle again?"

"Yup. Be ready." He hung up.

I beat my forehead with the heel of my hand. And I'd delivered the owner to the dealership so he could steal his car back. No need to mention that. And, there'd be no recovery check for me at the end of the month. Possibly no chance of a payment to the IRS.

Ouch, huh?

Note to self: never give a repo owner a ride.

I started the engine back up and struck out for my apartment where I carried the groceries up the stairs. Boss trotted from the living room to the kitchen and watched eagerly as I put the food away and filled his kibble bowl. Then I ate a hardboiled egg. Then some chips. Okay, a donut, too.

It was plain, not frosted, all right?

I threw away my napkin and opened my laptop. First I checked emails and was glad I did. There was an email from *Tow Truck News,* a blog I subscribe to, with the subject, "Repos Made Easy." I opened it and scrolled to the button, *click here to read the post.* I was all about *easy* and could use some pointers. Obviously.

My email shut down, then the word processor opened and closed before my eyes. Next the spreadsheet app opened and closed, then the photoshop app. I sat and watched as odd error messages floated across the screen. Suddenly the screen faded to black.

What the heck?

I squeezed my eyes shut and tried to pull myself together. I dialed up Axle and he answered with a grunt.

"I've been attacked by a computer virus. I clicked on a link and my computer went all wonky and now it's shut down. What do I do?"

"You opened a link? You know better than that."

"I know. Major goof." I could sense Axle's stare of disbelief over the phone.

"You need to install an anti-virus program. Make sure your firewall is turned on to block malware attacks."

"That's all good, but it's too late." I jabbed the on-off switch. Nothing. "Right now I can't even get the laptop to turn on." I jerked the power cord out of the wall and plugged it back in. Nothing. Fighting the panic gripping my chest, I said, "What else is there to do?"

"Wait till I get there and let me look at it."

"Wait?" My voice came out at shriek level. I took a moment to breathe and steady myself. "I can't wait. When will you be home?"

"I need a ride."

"You didn't buy that Altima?"

"No. It needed too much work, so I took a pass."

"Can you leave now?"

"Give me an hour."

I punched my phone to end the call and stared at my blank computer screen for a good ten minutes.

Too rattled to do anything else, I got in my truck and sped ten miles above the limit to Oberly Motors. I scrambled into the first auto bay where a teen in dirty, oversized sneakers and paint-splattered coveralls rolled out from under a car raised on jacks. It was my lil' cuz'.

He said, "You're early."

"Okay. I'll just hang out." I put two fingers to the corners of my eyes and blinked back some moisture. "I can visit with Byron for a while. No rush."

"Byron's not here. Shannon's gone too. They went to some meeting together." Axle sighed and climbed up from the oil-spotted floor. "I guess I can leave now. I'll come in early tomorrow to finish this."

"No, no." I did a palms up. "Go ahead and finish."

"Really, it's okay. I probably can't get it all done tonight anyway." He stepped out of his coveralls and hung them on a hook, then placed a couple of tools in the tall, red chest. He washed his hands at the sink, pulled the door to the auto bay shut behind us, and turned the lock. He strolled over to where I'd left my Fiat and I ran after him, dogging his heels, like a baby bear on the trail of its mother.

"You drive." I handed him the keys, got in the passenger side, and clutched the door handle all the way home.

"Yup, can't turn it on," Axle told me once he was in front of my computer. "You need a tech specialist. Call one of those repair services that removes viruses."

"How much is that going to cost?"

He lifted his shoulders and let them fall.

I swiped my phone to Will's number. He'd lend me the money to fix my computer as well as pay off the IRS, but that would come with a price. He'd tell Mom, then there'd be lecture upon lecture about returning to social work, even moving home to Denver. She loved me, but always forced me to put on a bright face and a positive attitude, because I would not admit to my mother that there was anything wrong. She'd go on and on about it if I did. So, I set the phone back down and found Axle staring at me.

I goggled at him. "What?"

"Just wondering what's going on in that brain of yours." Axle tapped the side of my head.

"I can't afford a computer breakdown." I not only owed Uncle Sam, I owed my mom a phone call or a visit, but not now. One look from Mother and I'd confess that my life was falling apart. And like I said, big mistake.

"I'll loan you the money, Delaney. I have some cash saved for a car, remember."

I gave him a *yeah, right* look. "I'm not taking your

money. What if a great deal on a car comes up?"

"All right, if you won't take money from me, how about Kristen?"

"No. Just no." *Ugh.* I couldn't ask my best friend for money, although I knew she'd give me anything I asked for, plus the shirt off her back. "I'll figure something out. How about dinner?" Food was a good distraction for both of us, and I had purchased a few more things besides junk food.

"No, thanks." Normally a bottomless pit, Axle surprised me. "It's Friday night, man. I'm getting together with the guys."

"You're not taking Shannon out?"

"Nah. It's gaming night. She's busy anyway." He vanished into his room to change and douse himself in aftershave.

After Axle took off in my Fiat, I sent a quick text to Ephraim to let him know I'd be busy tonight, pulled on a pair of yoga pants and an oversized tee shirt, and headed down to Roasters. I might not want to borrow money from my best friend, but thought nothing of borrowing her computer. My broken laptop was not going to defeat me. Instead of paying the IRS I would get my laptop fixed. Just watch me. In the meantime I'd use Kris's.

It was tempting to make myself an espresso, and maybe I would in another hour or two, but I bypassed the coffee machine and went straight to Kristen's cramped office in the backroom. I booted up her computer workstation and turned on the compact copy machine in the corner that also functioned as a scanner. I lowered myself into her chair and swiveled the seat side to side waiting for the copier to finish the series of hums and whirrs signaling it was ready.

Once the machine went silent, I got up to retrieve my cardboard box of receipts, but it was not where I'd left it from the last time I'd worked in the coffee shop. I peered under the desk, crawled around on the floor, and peeked behind the copier, but didn't spot the box anywhere. It wasn't in the storeroom or the washroom or in any other place in the entire coffee shop. I looked.

I raced up the stairs and hammered my fist on Kristen's apartment door. She must be out on a date with her boyfriend Zach or she would've answered. I texted her to call me asap as I slowly descended the stairs.

Kristen rang me back right away. I asked, "Kris, what happened to that box of receipts I left near the copier?"

"That was yours?"

"Yes! You didn't know?"

"I thought it was old paperwork of mine. I threw it in the dumpster. Tell me that was garbage, Delaney. Cause you know the dumpster is emptied on Fridays. That's today. That's why I took it out."

"Wouldn't you have shredded your papers?" I was holding out hope it was sitting somewhere to be shredded, waiting for me to rescue it first.

"I didn't think it was that kind of paperwork. Sorry, I should have looked more closely in the box."

My business records, the ones I needed for taxes, the receipts I needed for deductions, all gone...trashed. And my laptop...also trashed. You would think I had a backup of my laptop, but I never considered it. I'd had no problems with it before.

Are you getting sick of this? Because I certainly am.

I was too queasy to speak.

Chapter 8

Entering Roasters the next morning immediately plunged me into the scent of coffee. Nutty and cinnamon and normally comforting, but not today. Kristen was busy at the roaster and Guy was at the counter. The barista made my order then pushed the double espresso into my hands. I settled onto one of the highbacked chairs at the window and stared vacantly through the glass.

I couldn't imagine how things could get worse when DiNerdo walked in and things just got worse.

"Ms. Morran."

"It's Delancy."

"Have you got the—"

"—I know, I know. You're going to ask about the thousand and something dollars owed per tax code section two whatever." I glared at him through slitted eyes then turned my attention back to the window.

"Ms. Morran." He set his thin briefcase on my table. "Can you let me know where you are in the process? You have five days left to get in compliance."

I gave him the *what-the-hell* bad ass tow driver glare. "I lost my receipts. All my files. They were thrown in the trash by mistake."

His shocked stare bounced off my annoyed expression.

"And my computer crashed, too."

"That sounds like a poor excuse, like the cat ate my homework."

"Cat? It's a dog. The dog ate it."

"Well, I like cats." He would.

My accounts receivable mostly consisted of a download from my credit card reader. Rarely did anyone pay me in cash, but when that happened, I made a deposit at the bank. It wasn't the receivables, it was the accounts payable I would have the most trouble reassembling. I could recreate some of it, like my web hosting fee which is a fixed monthly expense. But I lost my gas receipts and all the others, and those added up to my biggest deductions. Not a catastrophe. Not total annihilation. There was a simple solution. Since I almost always paid for gas with a debit card, all I needed to do was go to my bank statements. That's simple. Not the end of the world. Easy-peasy, I tried to convince myself. Any other expenses not on my debit card I'd just have to forget about.

"I'll have my records back in order shortly." I did a brush-off flap of my hand in my best attempt at bravado. I could do this! I would do this! Trashing the receipts was not a big deal, I repeated in my head.

"Five days left."

"No problemo." I dredged up my bullshit gene, because that was a lie. Losing the receipts and all the time I had spent on them was a setback. Odd, though, that an IRS agent would make personal calls for a measly one-thousand-four-hundred-dollar overdue tax bill. It's likely costing Uncle Sam a heck of a lot more than that to have DiNerdo chasing after me. But, hey, what do I know?

After he left, I passed Kristen at the bean roaster and

threw the question over my shoulder, "Kris, can I use your computer again?"

"Sure. I have to email some orders this morning, so I'll need it myself in about an hour." She tapped the basket of beans with the side of her hand and the fresh roasted aroma shot out. I hadn't explained the importance of the trashed box because I didn't want her to feel bad. It wasn't her fault. It was mine alone. I should never have left the box lying around.

"Okay, thanks." I took my double espresso with me to Kris's desk. I summoned up my bank password from memory, and downloaded the year's debit card statements into a spreadsheet. I saved the file on Kristen's computer and emailed it to myself as a backup. Had I finally learned this costly lesson? I planned to return after hours when Kris didn't need her office. See, this wasn't bad, I kept reassuring myself. But it felt like I was spinning my wheels. How many times had I started this hellacious chore only to be crushed, killed, and destroyed?

After leaving Roasters with my double espresso in a to-go cup, I picked up my tow truck and buckled myself into the driver's seat. I inhaled the faint smell of motor oil and the woodsy scent that I imagined Dad left behind and pictured Del Morran leaning back in the same seat, his hands on the same wheel. It was almost like he was here with me, as if the tow truck was holding me safe in Dad's arms, like a vague recollection I couldn't quite grasp.

Not for the first time did I wish Dad was around to talk to about the business. I could use his advice. Would he just pay the frickin' one thousand four hundred bucks? Del Morran's too early death meant I couldn't ask, but somehow I felt reassured when I breathed in the faint aroma clinging to the truck's upholstery.

I took Pine to Fifth and Fifth to Main, then turned off at First, and six blocks later veered onto Eldorado Avenue. I was just trolling, but it paid off. At the corner of Eldorado and Washington, I happened upon a Buick Encore with its hood up—a standard front-wheel drive with an all-wheel option. I stopped alongside and leaned out my window to ask the driver, "You need assistance?"

The woman looked up from her phone. She was the athletic-looking gal with the short, cropped hair and a spiderweb tattoo on her neck, the one who worked at the store on Main that sold sports equipment. Her shirt was visible through the window, stamped with the image of a kickboxer and the words *Be aware, be ready, be alert.*

"You think?" The woman spoke through clenched teeth.

"I've seen you before."

"Yeah, so what?" Her upper arms featured some defined muscles, like she spent serious time at the gym instead of time needed at anger management classes.

"What's the problem?" I asked.

"I don't know." Her words were slow and clipped.

I gritted my own teeth and said evenly, "I'd be happy to tow you to your mechanic's shop so they can take a look at your car."

"Happy? I'm sure you are."

"I only meant—"

She barked out, "All right. Let's get going. Hurry it up." She opened her door and hopped out.

My face burned as I captured a photo of the VIN on my phone, but there was no indication of FW or AW for the drive shaft, so I asked, "Is your car front wheel or all wheel?"

"Don't you know?"

I bit down on my tongue. "I'll look it up." After buying a vehicle encyclopedia, after researching VINs, and after months of towing, I'd found a website with towing specs for every make and model. No one told me about this before; I'd found it on my own. I gave myself a mental pat on the back and pulled out my phone.

"Front wheel." The woman tapped her foot impatiently.

"Okay." I'd found the same information. I reversed my self-loader to the front of the Encore and pressed the magic button. *Presto, changeo…*the miracle claws swooped down with that metallic groan to capture the front tires and the hydraulic arm lifted the vehicle into the air. My truck never let me down and I found satisfaction in the routine.

"That will be $120," I said to the woman.

"This is highway robbery. Talk about taking advantage." She gave me a vicious side-eye before handing me her credit card.

"Thanks," I murmured with a tight smile. I ran her plastic through my reader and handed it back.

"I have someone coming to pick me up. Take my car to L&B Garage and Services and tell them I'll be there shortly."

I climbed back into the truck and snapped the gearshift into drive. She gave me a final scowl before I left.

But, hey! Now I could get my laptop fixed or make a down payment on a new computer. Or pay a hundred toward my tax bill. It felt like I was rolling in *moola*.

The phone rang through my blue tooth and I hit the

dash button to pick up.

"How's my favorite tow truck driver?" Ephraim's deep voice came over the line. A tingle traveled up my spine at the sound of his words and all thoughts of my annoying customer went bye-bye.

"I'm towing a Buick to the mechanic's shop. How about you, handsome?"

"Looking forward to tonight. You won't blow me off again, will you?"

"No way."

"Did you get a lot of work done last night?"

"Hell, yeah." Hell, no. But I can't tell Ephraim about the taxes I owed and all the time I wasted. That would be total face-burning humiliation.

"I'm taking you to the Cowboy Steakhouse tonight. Wear your best boots."

"What's the occasion?" My plum-colored cowboy boots with a swirly skirt would be super-cute.

"Missing you, that's the occasion."

Butterflies took flight across my belly, fueled by caffeine and compliments. After we agreed on the time for him to pick me up, I dropped off the customer's Buick and zipped home to get ready.

I took Boss for a quick walk at the park across the street, then went straight to my room. I yanked off the band to let my long hair out of the braid and shot into the shower. One thing about curly hair, you can't brush it when it's dry or the curls turn to frizz. It needs to be combed when wet, so while under the water, I applied a palmful of conditioner and ran a wide-tooth comb down its length. After rinsing, I stepped out and pressed a towel against the dripping strands. While I let the corkscrew curls air-dry, I shimmied into a short, pale-yellow skirt, tucked in a yellow plaid tank, and wrapped a wide belt around my waist. I squiggled my feet into my stiff cowboy boots. I'd just finished swiping on an extra layer of mascara when my boyfriend's knock sounded on the door.

"Wow, Delaney. I don't know how it's possible, but you look even prettier than the last time I saw you." He tipped my chin up for a kiss, and I closed my eyes when he lowered his lips to mine, then his lips moved from my mouth to my neck and back up to my mouth. *Yowza!*

When our lips finally parted, he said, "I suppose we should get going. I have a reservation." He pulled back as if waiting for my response, like he hoped I'd say our dinner could wait.

He seemed disappointed when I said, "Sure, we should leave," my skin still burning from his kisses.

He laced his fingers in mine as we descended the stairs. He was such a gorgeous lawman in his blue jeans and cowboy boots that he took my breath away.

The Cowboy Steakhouse was a fun place to dine. Inside the décor was all pine walls and hardwood floors and red-checked tablecloths. The air was redolent of savory meat and fried onions. A country-western band played on a stage in front of a dance floor. The menu was simple, with steak grilled to perfection and beer on tap. Our booth was in a dark corner where the music wasn't too loud, but where we could slip onto the dance floor if a song we liked came on.

After we placed our orders and the waitperson left a basket of breadsticks, a man and a woman entered the restaurant, catching my eye.

First my mouth dropped open, then the blood drained from my face.

DiNerdo swept across the room with a beautiful woman on his arm. He pressed a palm against her back and steered her toward an empty table where he pulled out a chair for her. He was dressed in his usual sweater vest and bow tie with highly polished wingtips on his feet; she wore a simple, sleeveless dress that showed off her long neck and slim figure. The awkward nerd stuck out like a broken flip-flop in a boot factory. The blonde woman was as put together as a perfect pairing of shoes with an outfit. She made my twirly skirt and cowboy boots seem plain in spite of Ephraim's appreciative looks my way. Could the nerd possibly be with this goddess? *No way! Not possible!* But when he took the seat opposite her and they held hands across the table, I had to believe the impossible.

I snatched a breadstick and gnawed on it.

Ephraim was telling me about his nephew, Maximiliano, and his antics of the night before. I loved his large family and the way they were all so close to each other. But I wasn't listening. My eyes kept darting over to the nerd and the knockout. When Ephraim finished his story, I let out a throaty laugh and said, "Excuse me, I'll be right back."

I boosted myself out of my seat and set out for the restroom. The door slammed shut after me, and I finger combed my long locks at the mirror, applied some glossy lip balm, then wandered back out to DiNerdo's table. "Why hello. Fancy seeing you here." Not original, I know.

"Ned, who's this young lady?" The glamorous woman's eyes twinkled.

"Ned?" I gave her a questioning stare.

"That's what I call my husband. Benedict is just too

formal. Ned is a nice sobriquet, don't you think?"

"Husband?" *Harty-har*. That's a good one. I threw an uncertain look at DiNerdo.

He ran a finger around his collar and laughed nervously. "I was called Ned as a child, but I prefer Benedict now. The only person who calls me Ned is Juliette." Good God, even the woman's name was beautiful.

Juliette gave her husband a gooey-eyed look. "It's our anniversary dinner. I waited years for Ned to ask me to marry him, and that's why I like to celebrate our special day so much. Isn't he adorable?"

More like adorkable.

Whoa, she waited years for him? I didn't see that coming. *Get out!*

I found my voice. "Ah-ah! Just as I expected. You're married." I blushed, thinking I just told a lie. Then I said, "Aren't you a lovely couple." Another lie.

I could hardly believe it. The two of them? Not a likely couple at all. And when I'd heard his nickname, Ned, I couldn't believe that either. Ned? Too much like Nerd. He must have been called Ned the Nerd when he was growing up; kids can be cruel like that, but I would never do such a thing.

"Well, I'll let you two get back to your dinner. It was nice to meet you, Juliette. Bye now, Nerd." *OMG.* I was a meanie after all. I sucked in a breath. "I mean, Ned. I mean, Mr. DiNardo." Heat flushed across my cheeks and I wanted to slap myself.

DiNerdo buried his nose in the menu and Juliette laughed, tipping her head back. She patted my hand, "You're a sweet thing."

Keeping my head low, I stumbled back to the booth

where Ephraim sat watching me. Our food had arrived and Ephraim was waiting for me before chowing down.

"Who were you talking to?" Ephraim wanted to know.

I squashed a groan. "Benedict and Juliette DiNerdo. They're on their anniversary. Do you want me to introduce you?" *No, please no.* I couldn't think of anything more embarrassing than going back to that table. And Ephraim can't find out DiNerdo's with the IRS.

He said, "No, that's okay." *Whew.* "We should let them alone if it's their anniversary." Ephraim sliced into his ribeye and red blood oozed out.

All my spit had dried up and my throat was parched after that awful conversation with Ned and Juliette. I took a long swallow of my microbrew before stabbing into my filet. Ephraim asked how my business was going, and if Axle had found the car of his dreams, and if Kristen and Zach were ever going to get engaged. My boyfriend was attentive that way, and I forgot all about the anniversary couple. It wasn't long before Ephraim finished his last bite and crumpled his napkin onto his plate. I would need a to-go box for mine.

Our song came on and Ephraim swept me out onto the dance floor. He curled me into him for the cowboy version of a slow dance. A table of women eyed up my man, and I wondered if he'd dated any of them. He'd been known around town as a player, working his way through all the single women before asking me out. Nevertheless, he made me feel confident now, although I was left with some uncertainty as to how long we would last. Those women had an eager look about them.

Insecure, much?

After our song finished, we danced a few more numbers, then Ephraim paid the bill. We were snaking our way to the door when we passed more familiar faces. Megan Putnam with the man I'd seen at her accounting office. She was wearing a sexy, red number, and the man was once again in a nice suit that went with his precision haircut and the stylish wave of hair above his forehead. So…was this her boyfriend? She'd called him Grayson, I remembered.

Ephraim halted, his feet planted firmly apart, and gave them a nod. He said, "Ms. Putnam. Mr. Thomas."

The man pulled back and grabbed his water glass. "How are you, Sheriff?" He gulped a mouthful of water.

Ephraim gave them his cop squint. "Are you two dating now?"

Not a single muscle moved on the man's face, but Megan thrust her chin high. With her red dress and startling blue eyes she looked like a woman in love.

After a moment of awkward silence, the man said, "We're just eating dinner together. If you have more questions for us, can it wait until later?"

Ephraim's flat expression turned into a full-on grin. "I'll call you tomorrow to set up an appointment."

The pair locked glances. Ephraim put a protective arm around me and ushered me to the exit.

"What was that about?" I asked when he opened the door of his truck for me to get in, my to-go box clutched in my hands.

"Grayson Thomas was the victim's boyfriend." Ephraim shut the door on my astonished face and came around to get in the driver's side.

"Emerald's boyfriend? Looks like he was pretty cozy with Megan."

"That's what I thought, too." Ephraim started up his truck. "Putnam claimed they were together at the time of Clark's death, but I haven't pinned down the details. One of the things I'd like to talk to Thomas and Putnam about tomorrow."

My mind buzzed all the way home with this new information. So, Grayson Thomas was Megan Putnam's alibi. And she was his. *Convenient, huh?*

A few days ago at the Chamber of Commerce meeting, Hailey, with the finance company, had mentioned Clark's boyfriend to Tanner. What was it she'd said? That they'd broken up, and that Clark's boyfriend wasn't too happy about it. Was it Grayson she was talking about? Was Grayson upset with her about their relationship ending? Had she driven him to Megan's arms? All good questions that made me curious.

I also wondered if Tanner knew something he wasn't telling me.

Chapter 9

The next day was Sunday. Since Roasters on the Ridge was closed, I felt no guilt when I walked inside Main Street Coffee for my early morning wake-up drink. The scent of the brew touched my nostrils and drew me in. After the barista, Violet, filled my order and I asked her if I could talk to her boss, Mike Horn, she gave me the go-ahead.

"Mike, you have a minute?" I asked when I blew through the door to his office.

The man in his forties, wearing a Main Street Coffee shirt and black jeans, with longish hair curling over his shirt collar, trying to look younger than his age, glanced up from his computer. He swiveled his desk chair around to face me. "Why there's little Delaney. Little Laney. You're looking fine this morning."

I ran my hand down my long plait, wishing I hadn't worn my red stilettos today, but reminded myself this was just Mike Horn's attempt to be charming and it wasn't a come-on. "Thanks, Mike. I heard Emerald Clark was your accountant."

"She was." His smile fell. "You asking questions in another homicide investigation? Again?"

I twitched a grin. "You spoiled my surprise."

He shook his head with obvious exasperation. "You're going to get yourself killed one of these days."

I held a hand in front of him in mock terror. "You

wouldn't pull a gun on me, would you?"

He quipped, "You never know. Why do you expect me to be so harmless?"

I snorted back a laugh. "Good one." But, did I know for certain he wasn't? "I heard the police took you in for questioning. What was that all about?" Nancy Abington had given me Mike Horn's name.

"Me? I was just one of many." He shook his head. "Looked like the police questioned a bunch of people, but I couldn't tell the cops anything. I know nothing about her death."

"Did you have any problems with her?"

He sat back in his chair and crossed his arms. "Nah. She did a good job for me. I had no complaints."

I sipped on my latte and studied him over the rim of the cup. "Did you know her very well?"

"Not really. She was about your age, not that I'm that much older than you." He chuckled and threw me an uncertain look, as if expecting to be contradicted. "I only saw her at the accounting office. She never came into the coffee shop." He raised his palms in a *can-you-believe-it* gesture.

"When was the last time you saw her?"

"I don't remember...at the end of the year sometime."

"Violet told me awhile back that you wanted to keep the coffee shop open in the evenings. Have you been doing that? Staying open till nine? Have you been working late?"

He leaned forward, his elbows on his knees. "Why not just ask me if I was working the night Emery was killed? You want to know if I have an alibi, right? You're about as subtle as a pink Corvette in a parking lot of black pickups."

"Ha, ha, I am?" I smiled and winced all at once. "So…your alibi?"

"For Monday night?" The man sagged back in his chair. "I don't have one. I haven't kept the coffee shop open late for several months now. Not enough customers. Like I explained to the police, I'm usually home by five and I live alone. Ask that sheriff boyfriend of yours, he'll tell you."

Ephraim probably would tell me if I asked. The sheriff was a good detective and operated by the rules—which is why I didn't have my thumb drive back—but he shared information with me if he believed it was safe to do so. I tapped my forefinger against my chin, wondering about that for a moment.

Mike's eyes opened wide before narrowing down to a straight line. "You know something? What do you know?"

I dropped my voice. "Only as much as you do, which is a big not-much."

"Too bad." He seemed to accept that, although he had a watchfulness about him.

"Do you know who Clark's other clients were? You might have seen them when the police took you in."

"Nancy Abington was there."

"Anyone else?" I found myself crossing my fingers.

He toyed with a pen. "Lena was there."

I don't think I know a Lena. "What's her last name?"

"Fields. Lena Fields."

Maybe the last name sounded familiar, but I came across a lot of people with somewhat common names like Fields either at the coffee shop or out on tows. At least I had another person to add to my suspect list. I wish it was being narrowed down instead of growing.

To make sure there wasn't yet one more name to add, I asked again, "Anyone else?" He paused a beat then shook his head. I thumped a fist on the door frame. "Well, I'm off. Have a good Sunday, Mike."

"You, too." He twisted back to his laptop.

I thought about Kristen's computer sitting idle in the closed coffee shop, but when I got back to my tow truck I had a message that there was a late morning pileup on the highway. And for the rest of the day most of the tow truck drivers in town were busy clearing the road, including me. I hauled a Chevrolet Equinox and Kia Sportage, both front-wheel drive, to the impound lot. The two cars were on all four wheels and easy tows. By four in the afternoon, I called it quits and motored over to the wine tasting room.

There were two couples I didn't know at the bar when I entered. Noel Yarborough, the vineyard owner, was in the middle of describing a bottle when his close-set eyes flicked to me. "Pull up a stool. Do you want to taste this Cab Franc? It's a blend of Merlot and Cabernet Sauvignon, a complex red."

"Sure. Thanks, Noel." I strode over and hitched myself onto a stool at the end of the bar.

Soon I learned the two couples were out-of-town tourists and knowledgeable about wine. We all happily munched on salty pretzels and snack crackers between pours. Both couples purchased several bottles before making their way to the door. Once they'd left, Noel scrubbed the counter so hard it glowed like my truck when newly polished.

I said, "I'm here to ask about Emerald Clark."

"I figured." He was of middle height, but easily

topped my five-foot-two from the other side of the bar. He studied me with his close-set eyes before pulling his gaze away to sweep over the now empty tasting room. "Damn it, Delaney, I had nothing to do with her death."

"I didn't accuse you of anything." Yet.

"Good, because I didn't *effing* do anything." He wiped his hands on a bar towel and tucked it into the rack. Noel's language didn't surprise me like it used to.

"I'm just digging around for info. Wondering if you have any clues." I tossed a handful of nuts into my mouth and crunched. At this rate I wouldn't need any dinner.

"I admit she was my accountant." He acted like this was news.

"Yours and just about everyone else's in town."

"That's right," he agreed readily.

"I might as well get to the point. Do you have an alibi?"

A cloud of anger passed over his face. "Really? I can't believe you're asking me that."

"Please humor me. I just want to eliminate you." And then I wanted to go home with a bottle of this fine wine.

He leaned his elbows on the bar and tapped the tips of his fingers together. "The tasting room is open every night of the week. What do you *effing* think I was doing?"

"You don't have any help?"

"Not yet. You know anyone looking for a part-time job?"

"I might. Kristen's baristas get off at three. A couple of them might be willing to pick up some evening hours, and I could ask them."

He perked up. "That'd be great, Delaney."

"Back to your alibi, did you have any customers that night?"

"I did, but none who bought any wine, so I don't have credit card receipts to identify them. Sorry I can't help you with Clark's *effing* murder. I don't know anything about it."

"That's okay. I didn't really expect you to. No one seems to have a clue." I took a moment to consider one last question. "Do you know anyone named Lena Fields?"

"Sure, I know her. Why?"

"Just a name that came up. How do you know her?"

"She's a customer here."

"Do you have an address? Phone number?"

"No. You don't want to mess with Lena, she'll kick your ass." His impatient expression changed to amusement. "She's pretty tough."

"I can handle myself." *As if.* After I purchased a bottle of the Cab Franc, I pushed back from the bar, and the soles of my red stilettos hit the floor with a sharp rap. "Talk to you later, Noel." I swung the door open wide as another couple entered and I left.

While in my truck chugging out of the parking lot, I glanced through the raised garage doors and found Noel staring after me. I doubted if Ephraim was able to verify Noel's alibi if he was alone. Same with Mike, who said he was home by himself at the time of the murder. And had the police talked to Lena Fields, my latest suspect? I asked myself how I could find out more about her.

Once back at my apartment, I worked on filling out insurance forms so I could get paid for the accident clean-up earlier today. It could take weeks before my invoices were processed. That's how traffic accident recovery worked.

I didn't complete the paperwork until about nine that night. Finally, I swept up my purse, my cellphone, and a heavy Maglite flashlight to head downstairs, but Boss beat me to the kitchen door and scratched on it. A high pitch whine came out of his muzzle, signaling he wanted to go out.

I left a note for Axle that Boss was with me. With the dog's leash in one hand and my purse over my shoulder, I locked up behind us. The Rottweiler nearly tugged me off my feet in his hurry down the steps, then he frisked around the parking lot working on his sniffing inspection. After he concluded his business, I unlocked Roasters on the Ridge, and Boss padded through in front of me, his nails clattering on the tile floor.

Roasters was dark and creepy this late on a Sunday night, like the place knew it had been empty all day, that it should still be empty tonight, and that I didn't belong. But now was a good time to take advantage of Kristen's computer, even if I was a bit anxious about being here alone. Axle's Rotty was protective company and the heavy flashlight I'd brought with me could serve as a weapon. Not that I would need one, but my Maglite and my Rottweiler made me feel safe.

Since I didn't want anyone who drove by to see any lights on inside, I kept the ceiling lights off in the dining area, but upended the flashlight on Kristen's desk to illuminate the inner office. I was careful not to disturb Kristen's coffee shop invoices and bills of lading when putting my hands on the computer keyboard. Boss gave a whole body shimmy, plopped down at my feet, and let out a contented sigh. I had all night to work in the silent space without interruptions, so I scrolled through the debit card statements I'd downloaded and highlighted my business expenses. I really should keep a separate business account.

At around midnight my eyes were dry and I could hardly keep them open, so I took the dim flashlight with me to the front and made myself an espresso. I filled a water dish for Boss in case he needed a drink, too, and followed the glow from the computer screen back to the desk to get busy again. My lids kept fluttering closed.

All at once my eyes snapped open. I must've fallen asleep with my head on the desk and Boss snoring across the top of my feet. Something had awoken me—a noise from outside. I listened in the dark silence for the sound to repeat, and Boss woke up, instantly on alert. Cold seeped down the back of my neck. I searched my hand around for my Maglite, but I must have left it out front when I made the espresso.

What did I have to be afraid of? This was the safe and familiar coffee shop where I spent all my time, first working for Kristen, then hanging around after I'd started working for myself. This is where I visited with my friends, drank my wake-up brews, and listened to Kristen's uplifting music while waiting for a call for a tow. The only difference was, now it was dark and I was alone, except for my dog, but I was always a little bit afraid of the dark.

A thunderous pounding on the door made me jump, almost sending me out of my skin. Before I even had time to get up from the chair, a man burst in, shining a bright light all around, and yelled, "Police. Don't move." He aimed his flashlight in my eyes, blinding me.

The police? Yay! I was saved. But what were the cops doing here?

My watchdog exploded into deep *ruff-rrr-ruff-rrr-ruffs* and charged for the door.

My heart stuck in my throat. "No! Boss, no!"

Chapter 10

"Stand down. Police." Sounds of canine claws skittering on the tile floor came to an end, and instead I could hear Boss's tail thumping. The officer said, "Oh, it's you. Good boy, good boy, there you go."

The bright light swung away from me and down to the floor. Boss was in full body wag, with ears perked-up, capering around Zach's ankles. The Spruce Ridge officer fondled the Rotty's head and tickled his ears. The silly dog rolled on his back for a tummy rub.

After a couple of seconds my heart resumed beating and my breathing returned. I flipped on the light switch. "What are you doing here, Zach? You scared me to death."

"Kris got a call that there was a dim light on inside. She thought there was a break-in and called me." Officer Zachariah Bowers was out of uniform in sweatshirt and sweatpants. With his prominent chin, handlebar mustache, and premature salt and pepper hair, he looked like a young Sam Elliott.

"Oh, I'm sorry. I left my flashlight on out front. I should have texted her that I was working down here. She said I could use her computer. I'm ready to leave, so I'll follow you out."

I went back to the desk and switched off the computer, then stood to the side while Zach locked the door. Boss stretched up his muzzle and sniffed the air, taking in the middle-of-the-night scent of dry pine needles, then scampered up the stairs after Zach. I trailed behind the officer and the dog. Kristen was waiting on the landing in a bathrobe and stockinged feet, with arms hugging herself against the cool night air.

"Sorry, Kris. It was just me."

She clutched at her heart, her eyes round with anxiety. "Dear Lord, I thought I had a burglar, so I called Zach." Her boyfriend would do anything for her, including coming out to check her store in the middle of the night.

"Sorry. My bad. I should've let you know I was going to use your office."

My friend stepped through her open door and motioned for us to follow her inside. Boss entered first, then Zach, then me. "Want some tea?"

"No, thanks." What I wanted was my bed. Her apartment was the mirror image of mine, but her décor was all black and white. Black couch, white sofa pillows, and black and white knobby afghan.

"I don't need anything, either, Kris. I should leave and let you get back to sleep." Zach rubbed her shoulder then gave her a peck on the cheek. He ruffled the hair on Boss's head, said, "Goodnight," and went out the door. My friend locked and bolted the door behind him.

"You really gave me a scare." Kristen sagged against the wall.

"Zach gave me a fright, too, but it's my own fault."

"You okay, Delaney?" She rubbed her eyes.

"Sure." Not really. "I should get going, too." I reached for the knob. Kristen had to be at the coffee shop at five in the morning to start the machines and stock the shelves and get everything ready to open by six. She was due to wake up in a few hours. "Sorry I disrupted your sleep, Kris."

"What were you doing downstairs at this time of night?" she asked.

"I needed your computer. I fell asleep down there. Stupid, I know. I won't do that again." I was a morning person, trained to be at my best in the early hours just like Kris, since I'd spent months helping in her coffee shop. The hour was late for both of us.

A kind smile creased her face. "No worries. You can use my office any time. You don't have to use it in the middle of the night."

I squeezed her hand. "Thanks, but no more late nights, I promise." I said goodnight and went across the landing to my apartment. I unlocked the door with one hand while holding onto Boss's collar with the other, but before I got the door unlocked, it was jerked open from the other side and my heart gave a jolt.

Axle stood in the entryway, hands on hips, eyebrows pinched in a fierce scowl. "You're finally home. I was worried about Boss."

I smoothed a palm over my once more thumping chest, at heart attack risk tonight. "I'm okay, thanks for asking. And if I have to say I'm sorry again I'll scream."

"Cripes. Don't get all bent."

"Sorry." *Argh!* I clenched my eyes closed and felt Boss's tongue against my hand.

When I opened my eyes, Axle had shoved his fists deep in his pockets. "What's wrong with you?"

The kitchen was in shadows only lit by the fixture above the sink. The refrigerator hummed its familiar tune and ice crackled as it fell from the ice maker into the tray. Boss smacked his tail on the floor. All familiar, homey sounds.

"I was working on Kristen's computer downstairs and didn't realize how late it was." I gave Axle a flick to the ear.

He gave me a bump to the shoulder. "Is this about the stuff you need for the IRS?"

"You guessed it."

"It doesn't take a genius to figure you out."

I gave up a ginormous yawn. "But I'm too sleepy to worry about the IRS right now."

"All right. Goodnight, Delaney."

"'Night, Axle." I retreated down the hall and fell onto my bed, clothes and all.

I was in a deep sleep, dreaming of columns of numbers that wouldn't add up, receipts that kept slipping from my fingers, and police banging on the door…when the phone rang. I went to throw off the blankets and realized I was sprawled on top of my duvet. Fumbling with the phone, I answered, "Del's Towing."

"I found that Hyundai Elantra. It's in the Ridgeside Condos' parking lot. You know where that is?"

"Patrick?" My bed creaked as I nudged myself to a sitting position.

"Yeah. You awake?" Patrick Crump, the repo agent for Abington Auto Sales, was the one calling.

I stared at the time on my phone. Four-thirty a.m. "Sure. You said Ridgeside Condos? I actually monitor that lot."

"Dankworth doesn't live there, but I got lucky. I was looking for another car when I spotted his. He probably has a girlfriend in those condos."

"I'm on it." Poor Clyde Dankworth was about to have his car repossessed again.

I disconnected and looked for a pair of jeans, then remembered I was wearing them. My hair was a messy tangle, so I wove it back into my usual braid while I searched for some shoes. Duh, I still had those on, too, a pair of black chucks. I hesitated at the kitchen door with my keys in my hand and felt around the bottom of my purse. Brass knuckles? Nope, didn't have those. Knife? Didn't have one of those either. Pepper spray? Yep. I shook the canister; it was active and that had to be good enough for this late night tow job. Clyde Dankworth seemed harmless. Right?

But I couldn't get my hand to turn the knob.

I knocked on Axle's bedroom door. "Hey, lil' cuz'."

A sleepy voice answered, "What now?"

"I have to go out on a repo."

His feet hit the floor with a thud and a moment later he jerked open his bedroom door. Axle always slept in clothes, so I wasn't surprised to see his hoody imprinted with an Indie band, his jeans slouched around his hips, and his stinky sneakers in his hands. We'd both slept in our clothes tonight.

He said, "I'm ready."

I said, "Let's go."

The night was pitch black, and the only lights to be seen were bleeding out from behind a few shuttered windows. I did that half-asleep/half-awake drive to go get my truck, blinking my eyes larger, like one does in the middle of the night, but the sight of my red Fulcan Xtruder locked behind the gate at Oberly Motors woke me up faster than a triple shot espresso. I loved my self-loader. Axle kept it washed and clean for me, and the red paint glistened under the street lamp.

"Where are we headed to?" Axle asked.

"Ridgeside Condos."

He leaned his shoulder against the passenger door and dozed while we traversed Fifth Street to Larkspur Avenue. I eased my truck into the lot and crept down one row of parked cars, then another. The truck engine purred. Cars filled just about every space. No wonder the condo association wanted to keep non-resident vehicles out of this crowded lot.

The Elantra, front-wheel drive, sat between a Toyota Land Cruiser and a Honda Ridgeline. The front of the Elantra was boxed in by a Chrysler Voyager. I thought about how to do the extraction for a couple of moments. There was no way to access the front end, so I'd need the tow dollies to lift the front and I'd use my truck to capture the back. I angled my truck up to the rear of the vehicle and brought out the wireless remote from the glovebox. Once I hit the button, the claws went under and around the rear tires.

Axle woke up at the sound of my driver's door clicking open. He slid out of the passenger's side and joined me to roll the dolly wheels out from under the truck bed. We pumped up the dollies without a word, each knowing what to do, until the Elantra's front wheels were raised off the cement. I hit another button on the remote, activating the hydraulic arm, and the car's back end swung into the air. Both front and back were raised; all the wheels were off the ground. We were ready to rumble.

I lifted my tired bod back into the truck and Axle settled himself into the passenger seat. My fingers curled around the steering wheel and I felt a surge of satisfaction. This was a repo job well done. A not-to-difficult extraction managed. No encounter with an angry owner. I turned the key and fired up the motor and listened to the grind of the engine, breathed in the smell of the exhaust, and leaned back into the driver's seat. Ah, the life of a tow woman. *Yeah-ez!*

"Oh shit." Axle's voice sounded alarmed. His eyes were fixed on a man racing across the parking lot in our direction. Clyde Dankworth.

"Shoot." I powered down my window and said to him, "Clyde, you tricked me. You stole your car back from the dealership." A good offense is the best defense, but I kept my voice low so it didn't echo against the tall buildings in the still of the night.

"Yeah." He smiled, his chipped tooth gleaming under the security lights. His eyes were in narrow lines, like he'd just woken up, too. His thinning brown hair was tussled and he needed a shave, unless that shadow on his chin was him trying to grow a beard.

"I'm not giving your car back." I attempted to pin him with a stern look, but I couldn't help feeling a little sympathy. He was only frustrated, not over-the-top angry like other repo'ed owners could be. "You know someone in the building?" I tweaked my head toward the gray condo.

He nodded. "I don't need a ride this time."

"I don't suppose you want to give me the keys?" I knew Patrick would appreciate having them.

"I don't suppose I do."

Axle snorted a laugh.

"Well, get in touch with Abington Auto Sales. Try to work out your payments. For real this time." I shifted my truck into gear, and Clyde waved as we turned out of the parking lot onto Larkspur, his Elantra trundling along behind.

****

I was dog tired on Monday morning. There's nothing as invigorating as fresh mountain air, as stirring as spring in the Rockies, and as refreshing as one of Kristen's fresh brewed coffees, but I was so drained I wasn't sure any of that would help, even caffeine.

The small line at the register moved along quickly. I took my espresso over to the table by the window and reached into my bag for my laptop. Bag empty. No laptop. I'd left my virus-destroyed computer on the kitchen counter. Not only had I forgotten it, I'd forgotten it didn't work. That's how frickin' shattered I was.

I took a final sip of espresso, then stood up and called out, "So-long," to Kristen. I dragged myself out to the parking lot. A black, one-ton tow truck with *Tanner Towing* painted on the door pulled into the parking space next to where I stood.

The tow man stepped down from the truck. "Laney, I'm glad I ran into you. Zach told me what happened last night."

"He did?" I drew a hand across my bleary eyes. Kristen's boyfriend, Zach, and my old boyfriend, Tanner, were friends, but why would they talk about me? Were they making fun of me? The tip of my nose turned red.

"Zach said you were working all night on something. What's up?"

I gave my head a shake and told myself to own it. After a few more seconds of self-talk, I said, "My computer crashed. I was using Kristen's to try to do some work."

"That's awful. I can't imagine going without my laptop. Did you get done what you needed to?"

"Still working on it."

"Are you going to get a new laptop?"

"I might have to." In spite of my foggy brain, I remembered I had a question for Tanner. "Ephraim and I ran into Megan Putnam and Grayson Thomas. Do you know who Grayson is?"

"He's a lawyer." Tanner stared down at me from his six-foot height.

"And he was Emery's boyfriend. And now he's hooked up with the other accountant, Megan."

His eyes went wide. "What are you saying? Are they the killers?"

"I don't know. Maybe. What did we hear at the Chamber of Commerce meeting? What did Hailey tell us?" I paused for effect and lifted my eyebrows. "That Emery broke up with her boyfriend and he wasn't too happy about it."

Tanner leaned against his truck with crossed arms. I wound my arms together, too, and joined him in relaxing against his door, comfortable together. A brilliant patch of blue sky shone between the pine trees in front of us. A flock of brown geese dotted the field on the other side of the pines. I relished the smell of the mountains and the fresh pine needles in the crisp air.

He said, "So, Grayson's motive is what? Revenge for being ditched?"

"Or, were he and Megan having an affair? Maybe that's why Emery broke up with him. Then her business partner and her boyfriend schemed together to knock her off."

Tanner drummed his fingers on his elbows. "That doesn't add up. If Emery dumped Grayson, and Grayson and Megan wanted to be with each other anyway, why would they kill her? There has to be a better reason than that."

"I know, darn it." I chewed the inside of my cheek. "What if Emery didn't break up with Grayson and it was the other way around. He kicked her to the curb, and she didn't want him to be with Megan. Maybe she threatened him. That might give Grayson a motive. Do you think it's worth questioning Hailey?"

When Hailey talked to us at the Chamber meeting, she seemed to know all about Emery's breakup. She certainly knew about my breakup with Tanner right after it happened a few months ago. Hailey was well known and knew everything that went on in this poky town. Maybe Hailey, the finance officer, knew all about Emery, the accountant, too.

He seemed to stare through the wall of pine trees at the edge of the lot and looked as if he was going to say one thing then switched to something else. "Okay. Can you talk to Hailey? Will you ask her?"

We were standing so close, Tanner's body heat radiated across the short distance and I could see his pulse thumping in his neck. My heart clenched with missing him. He definitely had masculine appeal.

I shuffled a couple of feet away. "Sure, I'll talk to her." Even though I suspected Tanner already knew something that I didn't. What was he not telling me?

"I need to pick up my sister from school for a doctor's appointment." Tanner extracted his keys from his pocket. I stepped back even farther while he pried open his door.

"Say *hello* to her for me. I'll let you know what Hailey says."

He gave me a curt nod. He was responsible for his

brother and sister ever since their parents died. His siblings needed him, and I just had to help him get the police off his back.

Tanner had left by the time I'd pulled my Fiat out of the coffee shop parking lot. Once I'd picked up my self-loader I set out for the smoothie place next door to Friendly Finance. Two strawberry smoothies in hand, I entered the office and plopped one on Hailey's desk.

"Morning, Hailey. Special delivery for you." I scootched a chair over and sat down across from her.

"Thanks, Delaney, I could really use this." Hailey reached for the cold drink. She sucked up a thick mouthful and closed her eyes. "Hmmm. This is so good."

"I ordered extra vitamin supplements for an energy boost. I need one today, too." I toyed with my straw. "Question for you. Just tell me to mind my own business if you don't want to answer, my friend."

Her deep brown eyes sharpened on me. "What is it? Are there strings attached to this smoothie?"

"Har, har. That'd be a big no." I took in her professional business suit, her chunky earrings and necklace, her manicured nails, her short, no-nonsense hairstyle. "I don't think you can be bribed."

She chuckled. "Well, if I could, this would do it. What did you want to ask me?"

I leaned my arms on her desk. "It's about Emerald Clark. Did you know her? I mean, were you friends?"

Hailey's mouth tightened. "I was wondering if someone was going to ask me that. I should've figured it would be you."

"Why me?"

"You've solved the last couple of murders around here." She dipped her chin and gave me an *amiright?*

look.

"But other than that?"

She rolled her eyes and made a speed-it-up, get-to-the-point gesture.

"Okay. I am asking a few people about her. Just a little informal investigation." I laughed.

"So, ask me."

"How did you know Clark?"

Hailey gave a little sigh. "I went to college with her. With both Emery and Megan. We were all accounting majors at UNC." A dark shadow passed over Hailey's eyes. "At first I really liked those two, especially Megan. Everyone wanted to be friends with Megan. She can be witty and fun. But once you get close to her, well…" She pinched her lips together.

"Well, what?" I pressed.

"Once you get to know her, you realize she sucks the confidence out of you. She makes snide remarks, never gives you a boost or a compliment, in fact just the opposite, and it makes you question yourself. It didn't take me long before I quit hanging around Megan."

"So, you'd say Megan is not a nice person?"

"She is not. She's judgmental. She holds grudges. She's uber critical." Hailey said that in disgust.

"What about Emery?"

"Yeah, about Emery, it was weird. Emery stuck with Megan like they were glued at the hip. Emery was needy, but I didn't know her whole story. They both came from Nebraska and went to high school together. I think Emery may have been estranged from her family and she depended on Megan like a sister. Just my impression. Like I said, I didn't know them before college."

"But it sounds like you knew both women pretty

well."

Hailey's gaze seemed troubled. "I guess I did once, but not anymore. After we graduated, they set up an office together in Spruce Ridge and I came to work as a loan officer here at Friendly Finance."

"So you kept in touch?"

"A bit."

"I was going to ask about Emery's relationship with Grayson, but maybe the more important question is her relationship with Megan."

"Well, Grayson seemed good for Emery, but I didn't know him. Even so, I thought it was too bad they broke up."

"You didn't know him? Never met him?"

"No."

"Do you know why they ended it?"

"I don't."

"But you said Grayson wasn't happy about the breakup. That's what you said at the Chamber meeting."

Hailey fiddled with her heavy, gold earring. "I didn't hear it from Emery herself. Megan was the one who told me, and I passed the info on to Tanner."

"Because Tanner's a suspect?"

She flicked her eyes up at me. "Yes, the police are focusing on him."

Tanner must have confided in Hailey for her to know this. Did he tell her more than he told me? The police had something on him, something he hadn't shared with me. Had he shared more with Hailey?

I swallowed that question and asked instead, "So, you must have talked to Megan recently, then?"

"Let's see. I probably ran across her at one of our meetings. We all belong to the Chamber of Commerce and the American Business Women's Association. I saw them more often at the Business Women's meetings than at the Chamber's."

I really should join both of those. "Did you hear about the skimming?"

Hailey's mouth dropped open. "What?"

"Emery was embezzling from some of her client's accounts. You didn't know?" I was surprised Tanner hadn't told Hailey about this.

"If I'd known, I would've reported her to the AICPA."

"What's that?"

"The organization that enforces ethical standards for certified public accountants."

"You'd report Emery even if you were friends?"

Hailey's fingers played with her shirt sleeve. "We weren't friends anymore, but yes, even if we were."

"So who do you think killed Emery?"

"Why Megan, of course."

Chapter 11

"Megan's the killer?" I gripped my smoothie so hard the strawberry blend shot up through the straw. I used my sleeve to wipe up the spill. "Sorry."

Hailey clamped a hand over her mouth and said behind her fingers, "I guess I shouldn't've said that. I have no reason to suspect Megan, other than the fact I don't like her." She drew a tissue out of a box on her desk and handed it to me.

I mopped up the rest of the spilled smoothie with the tissue. "Your opinion is important, I'd say. I'm putting Megan at the top of my suspect list."

Hailey rubbed her forehead. "Keep an open mind about the others, though. I don't want to sway you if Megan's not the killer."

"I haven't eliminated anyone. Hey, you ever run into a woman named Lena Fields at one of those American Business Women's meetings or maybe at the Chamber?"

"No. At least I don't think so. I don't know who she is." Hailey smiled broadly. "But you never asked me for my alibi." I'm sure my eyebrows shot up. She said, "See? You need to suspect everyone."

"Okay. What's your alibi for Monday night?"

Hailey tapped a finger to her chin. "So…Monday, Monday. I was in Denver. I had a stockholder's meeting with Friendly's investors. I drove down about five that night and got home around ten."

"Wow. Long day for you. And that eliminates you as a suspect."

Hailey smiled. "Don't you want to confirm it? Get the name of the stockholders? The name of the restaurant?"

"No way. Like I could ever suspect you." I flapped my hand. "Well, you might as well tell me. You know, just to be thorough." I wrote the names of a couple stockholders and their phone numbers on a page of my spiral together with the name of the restaurant. "Thanks for telling me all this, Hailey. You provided a more complete picture of Emery. I know her a teensy-bit better now." Not much, but a little. I shoved myself out of the chair.

"Stay in touch. Let me know what happens." Hailey waved me off and returned to her computer screen.

When I got back to my truck, I set my smoothie in the cupholder and wiggled into my seatbelt, but didn't fire up the engine. Hailey was right. I couldn't eliminate anyone from my suspect list yet. Like Emery's boyfriend. Hailey didn't know Grayson, but I thought of someone who might know him, or at least know about him.

I pressed the phone number for Will, my stepdad and my attorney. "Hello, Will."

"Laney. How are you, hon?"

"Good, doing good." I really shouldn't use my stepdad like this. Someday I needed to call just to ask how he's doing. And I still needed to phone Mom, too.

"You ready to send me your tax return and documentation? Just transmit your records by way of the cloud."

"You use cloud storage?"

"Delaney, if you worked in an office you would know how to upload records to the cloud and send me the link."

"I can do that, but I'm not quite ready yet." Mental forehead slap. I should've used cloud storage instead of a thumb drive in the first place. "Will, do you know an attorney named Grayson Thomas? He's about my age. I think he might practice in Spruce Ridge. He's dating someone I know," I added by way of explanation.

"I don't recognize his name, but hang on a second." Will paused a moment, then said, "I found him in the legal directory. He has an office in Vail." I could hear pages ruffling.

"Okay. Is there a way to find out more about him?"

Will said, "I'm looking him up online at the Bar Association now. He doesn't have any grievances filed against him, but grievances are rare, so I didn't really expect any." Now I could hear Will hitting his keyboard. "There are some online legal directories, too, and from those I can see that he practices mostly family law, like I do. But we haven't crossed paths. Is there anything else you want to know?"

"I guess that's it." Grayson Thomas worked in Vail in family law and wasn't in any legal trouble himself. It was a long shot that Will would know more about him. There are thousands of licensed attorneys on the Front Range. "Thanks, Will. I appreciate you."

"Sure, hon. Get those records to me."

"I'll call you as soon as I have them ready." I deposited the phone in my purse, but it rang right then, so I yanked it back out. "Del's Towing."

"Ms. Morran? It's Benedict DiNardo."

"Oh you. I mean, hello."

"I received information that you have more assets than you claim you have. I understand you have the means to bring yourself into compliance by remitting the $1,437.12 you owe per tax code §2.3104.141a."

My stomach did a flip. "But I don't!"

"I need to make an investigation into the allegation."

"Wait. What information? What allegation?"

"An anonymous tip. Please meet me at your place of residence. Now would be a good time."

"I'm not at home. How about in half an hour?"

"Fifteen minutes." He hung up.

His words left me shaken. This was an outrage. Who would rat me out like that? And what a huge hassle over this miniscule amount of money—not a large number in the scheme of things—although I didn't have it. I raced my truck out of the parking lot, but had to stomp my stiletto on the brake pedal when I came up to the speed trap at the curve in the road. Even so, I made it home in five minutes. I wasn't thinking straight, I was panicked, so I ran in circles around my apartment wondering what assets I had that would cause someone to report me to the IRS.

My shoes. My shoe collection was my most valuable asset. I had one authentic pair of designer heels I'd bought off a friend who purchased them with her employee discount. The others were knockoffs, but still, shoes are expensive and the cost added up. So I gathered as many as I could carry and sprinted to Axle's room. I tossed them in a heap on his closet floor and raced back to my room for more. After several fast trips, I'd emptied my closet and filled Axle's. DiNerdo had no cause to search my lil' cuz's room, right?

A rap on the door halted my running around and I

took a deep breath. I opened the door and tried to keep my voice steady. "Mr. DiNardo." *Amazeballs!* I got his name right.

"Ms. Morran." He stepped in to the kitchen.

I flung out my arm. "As you can see, I have no assets to speak of."

His gaze traveled over to the living room. The facing loveseats were fairly new, but not expensive. I had no original art on the walls except for prints of photographs I'd taken myself of the mountains and Kristen and Axle.

"The big screen television belongs to my roommate. You don't want to bother looking in his room." I tossed my thumb over my shoulder. "My room's the other way. You can look in there if you want, including the closet."

He set his narrow briefcase on the kitchen table.

"It's hard to believe you came all the way to Spruce Ridge to collect a thousand measly dollars."

"$1,437.12. But I didn't come to Spruce Ridge just because of you."

"You didn't? Is there someone else who owes you money besides me?"

"You're not the only one, but it's not me who's owed—"

"—I know, I know, it's the IRS."

"The Treasury Department. I'm not sure you're taking your debt seriously, Ms. Morran."

"Oh, yawn."

He looked startled and his Adam's apple bounced. "Now what's that mean?"

"I've heard it all before." So, he was here in Spruce Ridge for another tax evader, probably a bigger fish than me, like one of the celebrities with a mansion up the canyon road. The other guy must owe a much larger amount than I do to make his trip to Colorado worthwhile.

He adjusted his bow tie and swallowed convulsively, then cleared his throat in an irritating way. I wondered what his wife saw in him. Was it nerd-meets-popular girl? Socially awkward-meets-blonde bombshell? I've seen that movie. He coughed and cleared his throat again.

Would it be rude to ask him to leave? Yes, it would be. Mom taught me better manners than that. "Do you need something to drink?" I asked.

"Yes, thank you."

Why'd I have to be so polite? I crossed the kitchen over to the coffee maker. "Would you like coffee?"

"I'm more of a tea drinker."

Of course he was. "I can make tea. Is peppermint okay?"

"That would be nice." DiNerdo pulled out a chair.

Mint would be soothing for me, too, although my adrenaline was starting to wind down. I turned on the electric kettle and sorted out two mugs and the box of tea bags. I brought everything over to the table and sat down. "Your wife's *adorbs*, by the way." Way above him.

I was greeted by a blank look. He asked, "What did you say?"

"That just means she's pretty, you know."

"Yes, she is." He adjusted his pink bow tie, then took a sip of tea. "She came out from DC to join me for a few days. She's never been to Colorado before."

"I hope you're showing her the sights."

I couldn't imagine DiNerdo being much fun, but he went on to tell me about the restaurants they'd been to, and that he took his wife to the hot springs and up one of

131

the ski lifts to see the view. Talking about his wife made him seem a nicer person and less a nerdy tax collector. Before long he dabbed his mouth with a napkin and said he should be going.

There was something I needed to know first. "Who told you I had assets?"

"I can't divulge that. Informants are kept confidential."

"I have a right to know."

"There's no right to that information in the tax code."

How did I ever think he was a nice person? I rolled my eyes. "Oh, the all-important tax code."

He sighed. "But it's apparent your only asset is your tow truck."

A pit opened in my stomach and I clasped my hands in my lap to keep them from trembling. "Don't even think of laying a hand on my truck. I'll borrow the money from my parents. I'll get it for you." Yes, I caved.

He snapped, "It's not me you owe. It's the United States Department of Treasury."

"I still have four days left before the deadline. Four days, remember? I'm certain I'll have the money to you by then." This hassle would all be over soon and DiNerdo would leave me alone.

He stood. "Good day, Ms. Morran. Thanks for the tea." His face looked grim as he strode over to the sink and put his mug inside.

"You're welcome." I swung the door open wide and slammed it shut behind him.

Could the IRS really take possession of my truck? My self-loading Fulcan Xtruder was paid for. I'd inherited it free and clear. An asset to the business, yes, but more valuable to me than an asset. The truck had been my dad's. It represented my connection to him. What if I lost the truck? If I was a good daughter I'd take good care of his truck.

Threatening to take my truck brought out a whole new level of angry. Threatening my self-loader made me bat-shit crazy. Nobody was going to take that away from me, not even Uncle Sam.

Note to self: Call Mom and ask for a small loan.

I sank down on the couch with my knees crossed and my high-heeled foot swinging in agitation. I could just imagine how the call would go. *Delaney, move home. You can have your old room back. Save money while you look for a nice job*. She still worried about me like I was sixteen. Nah, I'll phone her tomorrow. I can put off Mom's lecture until I absolutely had to make that call. I had a little time left. Four days. I could put it off just a smidgeon longer.

Or, maybe I wouldn't pay DiNcrdo. Maybe I would continue to fight this. After all, a girl could change her mind.

My stomach got all squishy at the thought of risking my self loader. I would never take the chance, but I could take the full allotment of time to pay, all the way to the deadline.

A tow truck driver like myself is used to living life dangerously.

Chapter 12

"You have a minute to talk?" I'd caught Kristen coming up the stairs after she'd closed the coffee shop for the day.

"Sure." Kris worked the key in her apartment door and pushed it open. "What's up?" she asked as I followed her in.

"It's the IRS agent. He's such a pain, but it's not only him. All my customers lately have been especially crabby. More than usual." I tugged on my braid. "I don't understand it."

I thought back to the woman who preferred Owen Eckerd to tow her vehicle instead of me, the man who locked his keys in his car and yet insulted *my* intelligence, and that formidable, athletic-looking woman who wore a kickboxer shirt. She'd done nothing but complain when I towed her Buick Encore, front-wheel drive.

"Well, just because everyone else is being negative, that doesn't mean you can't keep a positive attitude." She stuck out a finger at me. "Remember, attitude is everything."

I pinched the end of her finger and shook it. "This feels different from the typical animosity against us tow truck drivers."

"In what way?"

"Not one customer has said thank you. Just the

opposite. Like, there's a lot of aggression out there. Most of the time people are happy when I show up after they call."

Of course, the people whose cars I towed from the no-parking zones were usually irritated with me, but recently even the ones who'd contacted me for help had been nasty. However, Kristen's advice was always good and I should ditch this downer attitude. Yup, she was in the right. I should be in control of myself. I shouldn't let others dictate my mood.

I said, "I've been meaning to run something by you. Noel Yarborough over at the wine tasting room is looking for part-time help. He asked me if I knew anyone. Since Roasters closes at three, I thought maybe one or two of your baristas might want to pick up some hours. What do you think? I won't bring it up if you don't want me to."

"That's all right with me. I admire employees who work hard. Just so long as a second job doesn't interfere with their job at Roasters."

"You want to talk to them?"

"No, that kind of lead should come from someone else. I shouldn't get involved."

"Got it," I said.

"Anything new with the murder investigation?" she asked.

"That? No."

Kris offered me a comforting pat on the shoulder. "The police will catch the guy." She stood beside me looking calm and serene as she always did, and I wondered what it would be like to be sure and confident that everything was going to turn out all right.

I never believed that. My adage? Murphy's Law.

Anything that can go wrong will go wrong, and at the worst possible time.

Maybe the problem *was* me. Maybe I did have a bad attitude and it was affecting everything, including how others treated me. I squared my shoulders and vowed that would change. Customers were *not* going to get the better of me. They were *not* going to influence my attitude. Ned the Nerd DiNerdo was *not* going to confiscate my truck. The police were *not* going to arrest Tanner. And the killer was *not* going to get away with murder. In fact, it was time to snoop around even more.

I asked Kris, "Do you know a Lena Fields?" Kris shook her head in the negative. *Hmmm.* Not many people seemed to know her. "Did you by any chance run into Anne Sullivan at church on Sunday?"

"Oh, yeah, yeah, yeah. I meant to tell you. I asked her about the accountant. She doesn't seem to know anything." She took a mirror out of her purse and touched up her lipstick.

"Shame that." I tut-tutted. "But, she told me she didn't want to speak ill of the dead. That sounds like she does know something." If Kris and I went together to confront Anne, I might be able to convince her to give up what she knows. There was no time like the present. "What are you doing tonight? Maybe we could go talk to Anne?"

She gave a sigh of utter contentment as she tucked the lipstick tube back in her pocketbook. "Sorry, Zach's coming by." As if on cue the doorbell rang and Kristen shot over to answer it.

Zach walked across the threshold and gave Kris a quick hug. They stared into each other's eyes.

I put on my brightest smile. "You kids have fun."

And with that, I took my leave. Kris was busy and I'd have to do the sleuthing on my own.

Back at my apartment, I grabbed my purse and my busted laptop. My last tow job had netted me a little over a hundred dollars, which should be enough to have my computer problem diagnosed. I zipped over to the tech repair shop at the mall and dropped it off. Next, I found a bench and sat down to call the sheriff. Actually, I found the bench after I walked through the shoe store. Okay, after I tried on a few pair.

That's when I called my boyfriend. "Hey handsome."

"I'm just about to leave the office. Want to meet for dinner?"

"I'd love to."

"Should I pick you up?"

"I'm at the mall, so tell me where to meet."

"My place."

"Great. See you in a few." I'd get dinner *and* clues out of him.

Ephraim lived in a brand new townhouse with all the new home features. Open concept, kitchen island, granite countertops, gas fireplace, vaulted ceilings. Very nice. The detail I liked best was the outdoor patio with a firepit because his yard backed up to the state forest. But inside there was only the basic furniture—a worn leather couch and club chair, a television that hung on the wall, and a bare minimum bedroom set. The rickety dining room table and chairs were hand-me-downs from his mom. I'd helped him paint the white walls an ochre color and framed a couple of pictures, but that's all he'd done to it.

When I got there I found Ephraim outside grilling steaks on the barbeque. My mind was filled with the smells of the outdoors, the aroma of the charcoal, and the sounds of the birds in the trees.

"By the way, what'd you call me for?" He set down the long-handled fork on the picnic table that held our beer, plates, and silverware.

I slipped my arms around his neck. "I missed you."

He laughed. "No really."

"Really." Legit. I was glad to see him. "I call you all the time, Sheriff."

"I'll take that." He brushed my hair aside to put his hand on the back of my neck and draw me into a kiss. I teetered on my heels but his other hand at my waist held me to him. Smoke swirled around our heads, so he released me.

As he stood in front of the glowing coals, I lifted one of his arms and slid underneath, settling in under his shoulder. I looked up into his face. "I did want to ask you about Emerald Clark's murder investigation, though."

His eyes flashed with amusement and he squeezed me to him. "Ah, the truth comes out."

I pretended outrage, my hand on his hard chest. "*Yeesh*. Okay, okay, you made me confess." Then I poked him in the stomach, but it was as hard as a rock, so I tickled his side. He tickled me back and I laughed until I snorted and my eyes watered. I fanned my face to keep my mascara from running.

He said, "I think the steaks are done. I'll be right back." He lifted me off my feet in a bear hug before setting me back down and disappearing into the house.

He made by breath catch in my throat. I mean, *dang*. The man was fine.

Once he returned with the steak sauce and a container of coleslaw, he took the steaks off the grill and we sat at the table with our plates in front of us. The savory scent made my mouth water.

I cut a piece and blood oozed out. *Delish!* "So, about the investigation."

"What do you want to know?" The sheriff played by the rules, and yet he didn't seem to mind discussing his cases with me, at least to the extent he felt he could discuss them, and he appreciated my input.

My eyes met his. "I heard a rumor that Clark was stealing from her clients. Can you tell me if it's true?" If it wasn't the truth, I needed to know.

"So, you heard that from Tanner, I suppose."

"What if I did?"

He took a second to respond, "All right. Tanner accused the victim of misappropriating funds. An investigation was already underway for embezzlement when her body was found. It's been determined that several of Emerald Clark's clients are missing cash from their accounts." He stabbed a piece of steak and shoved it in his mouth.

"Was Megan Putnam involved?"

"Not that we can prove," he said, talking with his mouth full, then he swallowed. "Putnam and Clark only shared office space. Their business entities were kept separate. We haven't heard of any improprieties with Putnam's practice."

"You'd tell me if there were any?"

He tapped a wadded-up paper napkin to his lips. "No, but I wouldn't have volunteered that there were none."

"Trying to follow that." I pushed the slaw around on my plate. "Is Megan a suspect?"

"Everyone's a suspect." Okay, that wasn't an

answer, and yet it told me she was a suspect.

He washed down a bite with a swig from his long-necked beer bottle. "One more question, then let's talk about something else. Otherwise you'll make me think you're only here for information." The corners of his mouth went up in a smile.

I pointed at my plate. "Well, that and steak." I wanted to ask him about the newest suspect, Lena Fields, but if I was only going to be allowed one question, it should be loaded. "What did forensics come back with?"

Ephraim set his fork and knife down. "There were signs that the perpetrator tried to revive the victim. Maybe the perp had some remorse, then panicked and fled."

"Really?" I set my fork down, too. "How about hairs and fibers and that stuff?"

"It was a dusty stairwell. But a water bottle was found at the bottom of the steps. It had the logo of a ninja on it."

My eyebrows shot to the top of my forehead. "So, does the bottle identify the killer? Is the killer a ninja? Who's a ninja around here?"

The sheriff laughed. "That kind of clue only happens on television. The victim's fingerprints were on the bottle. Likely she dropped it when she was attacked." He placed a hand on mine. "That's about all I can tell you. Are you done eating? You want to go inside?"

"Okay."

His big hand released mine and we carried our plates into the house.

I said, "I have some info for you." As I recounted Hailey's history with Megan and Emery, I loaded the dishes into the dishwasher.

Ephraim did the forehead wrinkle. "I'll question Hailey. Thanks for telling me they knew each other, Delaney, I appreciate it." His frown fell away and he put an arm across my shoulder to draw me closer.

His dimpled smile always made me melt. We didn't talk about the case the rest of the evening.

****

When I walked in the door of my apartment, Axle rose up from the couch. "What were your shoes doing in my closet?" he spat though clenched teeth. He was obviously in a snit.

I stopped short, gripping my keys. "What? Is there a problem?"

"What if Shannon saw them? What would she think?" His voice came out angry. Boss whined, sensing trouble in paradise.

I laughed. He was upset his girlfriend would see the high heels and think they were his? "You're pathetic."

He sniffed. "Oh, yeah?"

"Yeah."

"You're enjoying this, aren't you? You live to bother me."

"That I do." But I probably owed him an explanation. "The tax guy came by the apartment to check on my assets, so I hid my shoes in your closet. Sorry, I meant to move them back to mine."

His voice shifted from anger to astonishment. "Why would the tax guy look in your closet? And why would he care about your shoes?"

"As it turns out, he didn't." I plopped my purse on the counter. "I'll go get them right now."

"Already done. I moved them back to your room."

I gave him an elbow to the gut. "Thanks."

He rubbed his stomach where I poked him. "So the government's still chasing after you?"

"Like I'm an Amber alert."

He said, "Didn't Al Capone get sent to the big house for owing taxes? Not for killing people. Not for racketeering. But for tax evasion? I saw that on a TV documentary once."

"Oh?" I pretended nonchalance. "I'm not afraid of the IRS." I glanced at Axle to see if he was buying it.

"Whatcha gonna do, Delaney?" He shot me a worried look.

"Probably ask Mom for the money," I confessed. "But I'd like to make one last effort to get out of paying. Hopefully, the other accountant, Megan, will help me. I've asked my stepdad, too."

"No news on the investigation?"

"Well, Ephraim told me there was a water bottle found at the scene. It had a ninja on it." I just thought of something. "Clark was on her way to a self-defense class when she was killed."

"I guess she failed that class."

"Yeah, I guess she did." I picked my purse back up.

"Where are you headed to?" Axle asked.

"Downstairs to work on my bank statements. I'm trying to put together my business expenses." I was almost done. I just needed to go over the last month of statements. And, I needed to save my work to the cloud. I'm learning!

"I'll come with you." Axle snatched his phone and earbuds off the counter and followed me out the door. We stopped at Kris's apartment to let her know we were going inside the coffee shop, but she wasn't home.

The door to the employees' entrance opened

smoothly with my key. We skirted the stacked boxes of paper towels, napkins, and straws and made our way to Kris's office. The computer fired right up and I navigated over to the folder I'd created to save my downloads and spreadsheet. But when I opened the file, my heart sped up to the beat of the rap music thudding out of Axle's earbuds.

Horror must have registered on my face because Axle asked, "What's wrong this time?"

"I can't find the latest version of my spreadsheet. This one has only about half the information." We almost knocked heads looking at the screen.

He asked me, "Did you save your work when you logged out?"

"Duh, yes!" Or did I? I thought for a second. I'd zonked out, then Zach woke me up, and I shut off the computer when I was still half asleep. "Actually, I can't remember." I slapped my forehead a couple of times. "Oh, Axle, this is like one of those nightmares where you can't reach your goal. You're running and running and never make it to the finish line. I'm trapped on Groundhog Day."

Axle's eyebrows slanted down. "Delaney, just do it over. It'll probably go faster the second time. You'll get it done before you know it."

I had a *hand-on-hip, get-real* look. "I'll tell you when it'll get done. A big fat never. This is an epic fail. And it's not the second time, it's the third or even the fourth time I've tried to get this job done." What did I say about Murphy's Law applying to me?

His eyes opened wide. "*Woah Kay.*"

I rubbed my eyes with the heels of my hands. "Sorry, Axle. My bad. This is all my own fault and I shouldn't take it out on you."

He was quiet for a moment, then asked, "You going to be okay?"

I deadpanned, "Natch," then turned off the computer and said, "All this information is on that thumb drive I gave Emerald Clark. If only I could get that back. Her business partner told me the police confiscated Clark's files, so it's with the police. But what if Clark took the flash drive home to work on? What if my drive is at her apartment?"

His neck bent forward. "What can you do about it?"

I twirled the end of my braid with my fingers, thinking. "Get inside and look?"

"No way."

"Way." I thumped the desk. Axle aimed a laser stare at me and I volleyed one back.

He shook his head. "You're going to break in to the murder victim's apartment?"

"Come on. Use your imagination. Don't you watch movies? We could find the thumb drive *and* a clue to her murder." I snatched up my purse and keys and set off for the door.

Axle held up a hand. "Slow down. Take a breath. Chill out."

I'd already made up my mind, but stayed my steps. "Never mind. You're right. It was a silly idea."

My lil' cuz' trailed after me as I locked up the coffee shop. I waved him off and started for my tow truck which was parked in the far corner of the lot.

"Wait, Delaney." Axle caught up with me and pulled on the back of my shirt collar, jerking me to a stop, making me half choke.

My hand went to my throat and I sputtered, "What?"

"I'm coming." He popped open the passenger door, so I climbed in on the driver's side. He asked, "What's the plan for the caper, Super Sleuth?"

"Caper? Super Sleuth?"

"That's you. You've solved murders before. That's your super power."

"Harty-har." But I might as well explain my big idea. "It's late. Nobody will be around and I've got that slim Jim. If it works on car locks, maybe it'll work on a door lock."

"You know, that might just do the job." He clicked his seatbelt.

"Are you sure you want to come?"

"Crazy, I know, but I can't let you go alone."

"Sure you can."

"No way."

"Way." Axle looked resigned and determined at the same time.

OMG. We were really going to do this. I aimed the truck toward Ridgeside Condominiums on Larkspur Avenue. After I extracted my unlock kit from the compartment under the truck bed, I pointed out Emerald's balcony with the nice patio furniture and calculated the floor and number of units from the corner. We both tiptoed across the lot and up the stairs, as if it mattered whether our footsteps could be heard.

We counted the doors as we crept down the hall and stopped at her apartment.

I planted myself behind Axle to keep a lookout. Axle closed one eye as he worked the narrow ribbon of metal between the door and the wood frame. No one was around, so after a few minutes I crouched at his side to watch. He slid the flat strip of metal around so slowly sweat popped out on my forehead. I looked left and right but we were alone. Encouraging him to be quick, I made a speed-it-up gesture.

The lock clicked and Axle's hand hovered near the doorknob.

A mischievous smile crossed his face, then he nodded once, pleased, and I nodded back.

"You did it, Ax," I whispered. "Hail to the superhero. That's you, Axle."

"Jeez, you haven't got a—"

"Shhh!" I hissed.

Sudden sounds came from the other side of the door and we both froze. My pulse took off like a race car at the starting gate.

The handle turned and the door began to open from within.

Chapter 13

Grayson Thomas threw open the door, his eyebrows practically catapulting off his head. Axle and I shot up to a stand and Axle thrust his hands behind his back. Axle's eyes got really big, and I'm sure mine did too.

Since my lil' cuz' seemed to be shocked mute, I said, "Oh, hello. We were just wondering if anyone was at home. I wanted to ask about a thumb drive I gave Emery." I was smiling with twitchy lips, trying to conceal my pounding heart, and I expected my knees to buckle at any moment.

Grayson's forehead wrinkled, as if he was not totally buying my story. "Who are you?"

"Uh, Delaney Morran." I wasn't quick enough to tell a lie, and my mind may've even blanked my own name for a second or two. "Emerald Clark was my accountant."

"She doesn't live here anymore."

"I know." Heat crept up my neck and the tip of my nose turned red. "I thought she might have a roommate. Is that you?"

"No. She lived alone." He turned to pull the door shut with a slam. A click indicated it locked.

Axle and I shuffled a couple more steps back. I said, "Do you know if she brought any work home? Maybe my thumb drive is inside her apartment."

"I wouldn't know about that." He gave me a long,

level look, his legs spread, his feet planted. He was in his usual suit and tie. "And I'm not going to search through her things." Implying, of course, neither was I.

"Okay." I was embarrassed by the high notes in my voice. I asked, "You have a key?"

"Well, yes." I caught his hesitation.

Hang on. Just hang on here. Was he lying? Did he jimmy the lock like Axle had? Grayson was acting very suspicious and was rising to the top of my suspect list as the ex-boyfriend of the victim now seeing her best friend. He had motive, means, and opportunity. But what about an alibi? I asked, "Were you with Megan when Emery was killed? She told me you were together."

A look of puzzlement crossed his face. "No. I wasn't with Megan at the time."

There went Grayson's alibi. And Megan's, too. You'd think they'd get their stories straight.

"Aren't you two dating now?"

"Absolutely not," he protested. "We were together at the restaurant the other night only because, uh, I was comforting Megan. She'd just lost her best friend."

"I heard Emery broke up with you and you weren't happy about it."

"What?" His nostrils flared. "Why are you asking me these questions? Who do you think you are?"

My eyes went to the ceiling as I tried to think of something to say. He had me dead to rights. There was no way to explain myself.

Grayson said, all snarky, "You keep rolling your eyes like that maybe you'll find a brain back there."

Axle flared up at once. "You can't talk to Delaney that way." Although Ax talked to me that way all the time.

Grayson's hand shot out and he pushed Axle on the shoulder. *Yikes.* Was this man dangerous? Did Grayson shove Emery down the stairs like he pushed Axle just now?

I shouted, "Don't you touch my cousin," and stomped down hard on Grayson's right foot. Another reason to wear heels while out on tows or dealing with hostiles. Only these weren't heels, they were my stacked wedges that came down like a hammer on his soft leather uppers.

The suited man hopped up and down on his left foot, clutching his right foot in one hand. He sputtered, "Ouch, ouch, ouch. Damn, damn, damn."

Axle and I looked at each other and we both mouthed, "Run!"

We sprinted down the long hall to the elevator and I smacked at the button. Grayson pogoed on one foot in our direction as I jabbed the button repeatedly. Finally, the doors slid open and Axle and I darted inside. Grayson reached out and his fingers cut through the opening, but he snatched his hand back just as the doors crashed shut.

Whew! Close call.

I asked, "Do you think he can beat us down the stairs?" My voice was strained and my lips trembled. Okay, so I was a little freaked.

A bead of perspiration trickled down from under Axle's knit cap. The elevator smelled of new carpet, stale air, and Axle's sweat. "On one foot?"

We narrowed our eyes at each other, almost thinking in unison, *maybe...*

As soon as the doors opened on the ground floor, we cleared the elevator and bolted to the truck. I felt Axle's eyes on me as the truck roared out of the parking lot. I frantically gazed all around for a man springing after us, jumping on one foot like in a hop-scotch game, but Grayson had not appeared. He must've had trouble navigating the stairs after all.

Once we were a block away, I took a deep breath and let it out with a whoosh. "Narrow escape, huh, Axle?"

He made a derisive noise in his throat. His eyebrows hovered near his cap and his shoulders were stiff.

"I don't think Grayson suspected we were trying to break in. He was Clark's boyfriend, if you didn't know." I gave out a shaky laugh, but Axle didn't join me. "We certainly got away with it."

He puffed out his cheeks.

"All's well that ends well."

No reaction. Nothing. Nada. He didn't utter a word. Was he having a breakdown?

A car horn blared from behind me and I realized we'd been sitting through a green light. I gave the truck some gas and went through the yellow, leaving the horn honker behind at the red. My hands were sweaty on the steering wheel. "Axle, are you mad at me?" I could take his teasing, his insults, his jabs, but I'd die if Axle was angry with me. We're like family now.

"I should be for letting you talk me into this." The boy speaks!

"You insisted on coming."

He reached inside his hoody and jerked out the slim Jim. "You can have this back since the fun's over."

I jumped on that. "It was fun, wasn't it? You're the superhero, not me. It was a caper, right? Come on, you had that door unlocked. You did it! You really did it!"

"Don't remind me, Super Sleuth. What if I'd opened

the door and that man caught us doing a B&E?" Axle rubbed a spot over his heart.

"But he didn't catch us."

"Almost."

"But he didn't."

"He was going to beat me up. Look, you're supposed to be the adult here. You're supposed to be the one talking sense into me. When did we reverse roles?" Axle belched. "I think I need an antacid."

"Look in the glove compartment, grandpa." Hysterical laughter bubbled in my throat. But he was right and I was a bad friend. I clamped a hand over my mouth to curb the urge to laugh. "I'll never, ever talk you into anything like that again, I promise."

Axle shook out a couple of antiacids from the bottle. "So, I'm the superhero?" He had on a slight smile.

"Yes, you are."

"This was all totally your fault, by the way."

"Yes, it was."

"Fine," he smirked and I started to feel we were getting back to normal. I parked the truck in the secure corner of the dark lot at Oberly Motors and we climbed into the Fiat. The closer we got to our apartment, the more surreal the attempted break-in became. Did we actually risk committing a felony? Even though superheroes did it all the time in the movies. Once I'd parked the Fiat at the apartment, I pulled the keys from the ignition and we got out.

"So, I'm a superhero?" Axle asked again, striking the classic pose, shoulders squared, elbows out, arms flexed at his sides with his hands fisted. He stood in a circle of light from the halogen lamppost.

"And I'm Super Sleuth." I lowered one knee and one

hand to the ground, with my other leg splayed straight out, in a typical cartoon position.

Axle put his hands on his hips and stuck out his chest trying to pump himself up. I shot to my feet and did a kickboxing thingie. "What kind of super powers do I have?" I asked the teen expert.

"Just persistence, you know, being a pest, very annoying."

I did a couple more kicks and fake karate chops on the way up the stairs and growled like a badass dude.

Kristen materialized on the top step, seeming to come out of nowhere. My growl turned into a shriek, "*Aieeeeee!*"

"Dear Lord," Kris screamed, clutching her shirt front.

I almost keeled over. "Sorry, but you scared me."

Axle said, "So much for the brave and awesome Super Sleuth."

"You scared me, too," Kristen said.

I wrapped my arms around my best friend and patted her back. "You okay? What are you doing out here?"

"I was looking out the window and happened to see the two of you acting weird. You were, like, on the ground, then you were standing up and kicking. So I came out to meet you on the stairs."

How to explain it? Axle and I were just having fun, but I guess it would appear bizarre. My little cuz' and I exchanged amused looks.

I said, "We were just playing around." Her gaze darted to our guilty faces. I asked her, "It's late, shouldn't you be in bed?"

She bobbed her head in agreement. "See you tomorrow," before retreating into her apartment.

"Get a good night's sleep," I told her as she disappeared.

Axle and I stumped through our door and parted ways to head to our rooms. "Sleep tight," I said to my lil' cuz.

"I will. You do the same."

But, I didn't manage to. I tossed and turned and tried to sleep. I might talk a big talk to Axle, act all tough like a superhero, but I'd been pretty intimidated by that man. In my dreams we were still at the door, trying the lock, hiding the slim Jim, running from a hopping-mad man in a gray suit.

****

A call came in for a tow the next day at mid-morning, so I raced to pick up my truck and zoomed over to Main and Fifth where my customer's car was stalled. When I was still a few blocks from the corner, I passed Owen Eckerd's ugly green wrecker going the other direction. He glared at me through his open window when our tow trucks passed each other. By the time I arrived at my destination, I'd erased the scowl from my face and replaced it with a smile. Attitude! Kristen told me to work on my attitude. Remember? Forget Murphy's Law and think positive thoughts.

The Kia Forte, front-wheel drive, blocked the turn lane in the busy intersection, not a good spot for a breakdown, causing drivers to throw angry looks as they maneuvered around the gridlock. I pulled up behind the Kia, flipped the light bar on, and shrugged into my orange safety vest. Wouldn't you know it, my choice of footwear today was a melon-colored pair of lace-up gladiator sandals, a warm orange for a positive outlook. *Matchy-matchy.*

"Hello. I see you're in a bit of trouble here." I offered him my most upbeat smile and my hand to shake.

The man asked, "What are you laughing at?" and my grin froze. He said, "There's nothing funny about this." As if to emphasize the point, a passing motorist leaned out his window and made a rude hand gesture.

I felt heated to the roots of my hair and knew my neck had turned blotchy, too. "Right. Why don't you get what you need out of your car and wait on the corner for me to hook up?"

"Why don't you get a move on?" His face was a picture of fury and his voice held an imperious tone.

It took restraint not to react to Mr. Angry Man. Attitude! I favored him with another smile. "After I move the car, I'll pull around to the corner and you can get in the truck."

"Fine." He opened his driver's door and two seconds later slammed it shut.

While he crossed the street with his head down, I went back to my self-loader and waited for the traffic signal to turn green, then pulled around in front of the Kia and backed up. Now it was my truck that blocked the intersection, but not my problem. I tapped the button on the wireless remote to operate the T-Bar and lower the claws to the ground. The claws hadn't lined up with the wheels, so I backed up another foot, then pressed a second button. The Kia rose in the air, secure in the metal arms of my self-loader. The light had switched to red, so I looked both ways before proceeding through with the Kia on the back. After clearing the intersection, I slid the truck up to the opposite curb, the Kia fitting in behind. My customer was not waiting for me as I'd asked him; he was nowhere in sight. I made certain all my flashing lights were on and popped my door open, sliding my gladiator sandals to the ground.

Behind my dark sunglasses, I scanned up and down the busy street. Tourists lined the sidewalks on Main, clutching shopping bags, to-go coffees, and cellphones, ready to take pictures of the scenery in this mountain town. There were plenty of motor vehicles and bicycles and pedestrians, but no Mr. Angry Man. Where in the world had he gone off to? My text to the number he'd called from received no response. I had no idea where he wanted me to deliver the Kia, or I would've just left him behind and taken off. I leaned against the back of my truck, trying to look like a professional vehicle recovery agent. In reality I was trying to keep my cheeks from aching from the smile I'd plastered on my face. Attitude!

I reminded myself I was living the dream, being my own boss, helping people even if they didn't appreciate it, working in this small, picturesque town, the gateway to the mountains and ski resorts. That took up about five seconds. Next, I scrolled on my phone and exchanged my screen saver pic for a pair of tall black boots, the kind a superhero would wear.

Ten or so minutes later, my customer walked out of Main Street Coffee with a drink and muffin in his hands. I waved for him to hurry over, but he ignored me, taking his sweet time strolling up to the truck.

"There you are." I opened the passenger door and he climbed in. "Where to?" He gave me the name of his mechanic's shop. It would be L&B Garage and Services, my least favorite garage in town, and I trundled his Kia over there. I got the last laugh, though, since I charged him an extra ten bucks.

"Why did you call me for a tow? Did someone refer

you?" I asked as I handed him back his credit card.

"You're the cheapest in town. The other two I called were going to charge fifty bucks more." He had on a smug look.

I squelched the urge to slap his face. "Thank you for using Del's Towing." I fumed as I peeled out of the lot, my red-hot face reflecting my red-hot anger. No more positive attitude. Forget that.

Five minutes later I was inside Roasters, hoping no one would notice the high spots of color on my cheeks. I peered all around to make sure Nerd the DiNerdo wasn't nearby. Guy had my double espresso ready when my turn came up at the cash register.

"Thanks, Guy." I paid him and stuffed a tip in the jar. "I was talking to Noel Yarborough over at the tasting room the other day, and he told me he's looking for part-time help if you're interested. You can tell the other baristas, too."

"Okay. I might look into that." He cleared out the wand on the espresso machine with a whoosh of hot air and rubbed a wet towel over the metal.

I started to duck into the backroom, when Axle came through the door. I said, "Hey, Axle." He ignored me and got in line, then I noticed the tell-tale earbuds, so I slapped him upside the head to get his attention. "Hey, Axle. What are you doing here? Why aren't you at work?"

He pulled the buds from his ear. "Making a coffee run."

"Join me in Kristen's office before you leave?"

"K." He moved forward in the line.

I went to find Kristen who was in the stockroom doing inventory, which told me she was about to place an order and would be needing her office. "Can I get on your computer real quick? It won't take but a minute."

"Of course, Delaney." She made a mark on her checklist without turning around.

"Thanks." I ran for her cramped office and fell into her chair.

It didn't take long for Axle to waltz in with a full tray of drinks and set them on the filing cabinet. He glanced between me and the office computer. "Did you ever get your laptop up and running?"

"Nope. It's at the repair shop."

"So, whatcha doin? Working on your spreadsheet?"

"No time. I'm looking up my suspects on social media." I typed Grayson Thomas's name into the query and his picture popped up. He was wearing a suit in the photo. Didn't the guy ever go casual? "Remember him?"

"Huh. Can't forget that dude. Did you need me for something?" He scratched the back of his neck.

I turned to answer him over my shoulder. "Can you keep a lookout for me? Let me know if Ned DiNerdo comes into the coffee shop. The IRS guy."

"He won't come back here."

I arched my brows. "He won't, won't he? Can you guarantee that?"

"O-kaaay." Instead of going to check, he leaned in. "That guy's page is private. You're not going to find a lot other than his profile pic."

"Yeah, I noticed." I clicked around to another site with a hit on Grayson Thomas' name. I didn't care if I was creeping him online. But there wasn't much to discover, only his name mentioned in his firm's advertisement. The guy probably knew better than to post anything on the internet. The search on Lena Fields yielded too many results so I added Spruce Ridge to the query. The sporting goods store's website opened to reveal a photo of her.

"Who's that?" Axle asked.

"Another of Clark's clients."

She had uber short hair and no makeup, but was attractive with high cheekbones and a pointed chin, and on her neck was the spiderweb tattoo. The motto, *It's not violence if it's self-defense*, was across the top banner on her webpage. Several other photos showed her kickboxing or in some other kind of contact sport.

I knew this woman.

I knew Lena Fields.

Now I could place a name to a face.

I'd run across her several times before. The sporting goods store on Main Street. And I'd towed her Buick Encore, front-wheel drive, from Eldorado and Washington Street. That's why her name was familiar. I'd seen it on her credit card. She was a mean customer then and looked like a mean customer now.

"How about the dead lady, the accountant? Did you query her?" Axle hovered over my shoulder.

"Yeah. There's nothing for Emerald Clark except the Spruce Ridge Accounting website and a private social media account." I chewed the inside of my cheek. "Same for Megan Putnam. They've followed the same *MO*. Seems like everything's private. The company website didn't have any testimonials from satisfied customers. I sure wish I could get the names of all Clark's clients because the killer could be on her client list."

Axle murmured a low *hmmmmm*. "I'd better get these drinks back to Byron or he'll wonder what the heck happened to me."

"Is there a drink for Shannon there, too?" I formed a heart with my hands and made kissy sounds.

He gave me a heavy sigh. "You're one of those."

"Those what?"

"Hopeless rom-com addicts."

"Well, I, um." The little twerp was right. "Will you make sure DiNerdo's not out front before you go?"

He left and I quickly scanned the news articles online about Emerald Clark's death. Nothing new there or in the news release at the Sheriff's Department.

Axle returned. "Coast's clear."

I closed the search tab on Kris's computer and followed him to the front, then we both walked out of the coffee shop together. Axle set the drink tray in the passenger seat of Byron's loaner car before he buckled himself in the driver's seat and took off.

I jumped into my tow truck, took Pine to Main Street, and slammed to a stop in front of the sporting goods store. The aisles of workout clothes and equipment were empty of bargain hunters and the man behind the checkout said Lena was not working today.

Leaving Main Street behind, I cut across Front Street to the three-story, redbrick building that housed Spruce Ridge Accounting. I idled my truck in the lot with my foot on the brake. Megan had lied about her alibi, if Grayson was to be believed, and they were both concealing something, of that I was sure. And who doesn't use social media? *Amiright?* Neither of them had much of a presence on the internet. Very irregular if you ask me.

I tapped on my phone again and looked up Sullivan's Flower Shop, then punched my orange gladiator heels on the gas.

The bell dinged when I walked through the door. Anne Sullivan sold not only flowers, but all sorts of knick-knacks and kitsch. Hummingbird windchimes, angel statuary, garden flags, and ugly gnomes. She was buttoned up with a customer, so I perused the sun catchers and bird feeders until the shopper left.

"Anne, remember me?" I approached the checkout. Several donation cans crowded the counter, filled with bills to help save the wolves, benefit an animal shelter, and provide veterinary services for wild horses. Seems like she cared about animals.

She met my steady gaze. "From the Chamber meeting, of course."

I absently touched the thick braid twisted over my shoulder. "I need a little bereavement gift."

"One of these succulents in the ceramic pots would be nice." Anne waved to a stand near the counter that held colorful round pots with various cacti and prickly plants.

"Perfect." I picked out a yellow flowering cactus in a miniature green pot and handed it to the flower seller. "I'm buying this for Emery Clark's business partner, Megan."

"This is nice and cheerful." Anne nodded and placed the pot in the bottom of a brown paper bag with handles. The bag was stamped with a hummingbird drinking from purple blooms and the name of the shop, "Sullivan's Flowers."

I extracted my debit card from my wallet and reshouldered my purse. "Do you know Kristen Guttenberg? She goes to your church."

Anne thought for a moment, then her face lit up. "Oh

sure, I know Kristen. Real nice young lady. Receipt in the bag?" She rang up the sale on an old-fashioned cash register, not on a device with a card reader.

"I'm a good friend of hers," I said with enthusiasm. "I'll take the receipt." She handed it to me and I tucked the paper into my purse.

"I just talked to her the other day." The woman gave me a genuine smile. "Small world, isn't it?"

"Sure is. That's why it's not surprising everyone used Emery Clark as their accountant. Or Megan Putnam. Same office." I held my hand out for the bag. "I'm taking this over to Megan right now."

"So you were friends with them?"

"Not really. But it's the right thing to do. Have you sent any flowers?" I gave the shop around me a meaningful glance. I'm using the do-gooder-shaming ploy, God don't strike me down.

She looked uncertain. "I haven't heard about a funeral."

"I'll find out and let you know." I shifted my stance, uncertain as to my next question. "You said you didn't want to speak ill of the dead, but I'd sure appreciate it if you could tell me what you know about Emery… I'm just trying to be helpful and all…and since I'm a friend of Kristen's…"

"Well…" Anne cast her eyes down.

"I'll keep whatever you say between the two of us." I made the standard zipping motion over my lips.

"I guess this is all going to come out in the investigation anyway."

"That's right," I agreed, trying not to smile too broadly.

"Okay, if it's for a good cause."

"It is." The good cause was to help myself solve the case and get my thumb drive back.

She leaned in close. "I never suspected a thing before all this happened, but after her death I looked over my statements, and there's a large sum of money missing from my bank account." Her voice came out almost as a whisper, as if she was ashamed to tell me this.

Yowza! Bingo!

"You didn't know before she died?" I asked.

She shook her head.

"You didn't have a motive, then." She looked alarmed, so I added, "Not that anyone would suspect you."

"No, but the police asked me so many questions I almost felt like confessing." For a moment she did look guilty.

"That's awful. But you told them your alibi, didn't you?"

"Yes. I was home all night with my husband watching our new grandbaby." Anne whipped out her phone and showed me a picture.

"*Oooh*, look how cute," I cooed. Anne sat next to a man about her age with a little bundle of joy in her arms. Sure did look like she had an alibi, but how did I know when the photo was taken? The police can check the date stamp, because that cannot be faked on a digital camera. Too bad I'm not with the police.

She slid the phone back into her pocket. "The family might call me about the funeral since I do flowers for a lot of the services around town."

"I'll try to find out when the funeral is," I assured her. I pulled out one of my handy Del's Towing cards. I said, "Let's stay in touch."

She took the card. "Okay."

The door closed behind me with a *ding-a-ling*. This grandma could not be the killer. But I planned to ask Ephraim if he verified her alibi just the same.

Back in my truck, I returned in a matter of minutes to the redbrick building on Front Street.

Chapter 14

I stepped into the accounting office to an empty waiting room with no receptionist. The aquarium gurgled, but other than that there was no sign of life. So, without anyone here to help me, I called the business number and heard the phone ring on the other side of the door.

Megan answered, "Spruce Ridge Accounting."

"Hello. It's Delaney Morran. Do you have a minute to talk? I'm in your waiting room."

"You're in the office?"

"Yes."

"All right." I could practically hear her disapproval over the phone.

"Sorry I didn't call ahead for an appointment," I said when Megan flung the door open.

"You might as well come on back." She led the way to her office and parked herself behind her desk. "What can I do for you?"

I took the seat across from her. "Can you tell me if there's going to be a funeral?"

Megan's illuminous blue eyes showed some surprise.

I added, "Please."

She hesitated a moment, then said, "Emery's mom is arranging to have the body cremated. No service except for immediate family and that's back in

Nebraska."

"Her family was close?"

"Actually, no. But her mom came forward to take care of the arrangements. They may have had their problems, but she's her mom after all."

So, I couldn't check out suspects at a graveside service. That was a longshot anyway. I asked, "You're okay with that?"

"Sure. Family is family." Megan sniffed, took a tissue from the box on her desk and touched it to her nose.

"Totally." I blinked at the water forming in the corner of my own eye. My mother would take charge if something happened to me. But then, my mom and I are tight-knit in spite of driving each other crazy.

Note to self: give Mom a call.

I set the Sullivan Flower Shop bag on Megan's desk. "This is for you."

She peeked in the bag, then brought out the potted cactus. "Thank you. Usually people send flowers, but this itty-bitty cactus is a nice change. I'll find somewhere to put it." She looked at it from all angles, then set it on the credenza behind her, basically out of sight. She gave me a hard look. "But you're here for more than this."

I said, "I'm struggling to get my records together and I really need my thumb drive."

She rested her elbows on the edge of her desk. "I can't help you there. The police haven't released Emery's files."

"Did you look for my thumb drive in her office?" I asked in a slightly pleading tone.

"No need. The police have it. We've been over this before. Or did you forget, like you forgot where you put your records?"

"I didn't forget...never mind." I crossed my arms and leveled my gaze at her. "Will you at least answer some questions for me?"

She blinked and darted a glance around. "About what? Haven't I been answering your questions?"

"Yes. And I appreciate it, but I'm wondering about Emery's enemies. Do you know if anyone threatened her?"

She pointed her crystal blue gaze toward me. "Don't you think the police already asked me that?"

"I just want this murder solved so I can get my flash drive back, all right?" There. She knew the truth about me. I was self-centered and petty. My face scorched hot and I really wanted to avoid such negative self-assessments in the future. "I'm sorry. I know she was your good friend."

"Yes, she was. Some of her clients may've been upset, as you and I already discussed, but I don't think they'd count as enemies." She tented her fingers.

"So not upset enough to kill her?"

"I guess I can't answer that."

"You have an alibi, don't you Megan?" I wanted her side of the story. Was she still counting on Grayson to alibi her or had she come up with something else?

She cringed back in her chair and placed a hand over her heart. "Me? Yes, I do." I shrugged in *a what-can-I-say* gesture. After a tense moment, she told me, "I was out with Grayson Thomas that night."

"A restaurant? A movie?" I pressed.

"No, at my place." A smile lit up her face for a second before it was gone.

"Grayson said he wasn't with you that night."

She stiffened her spine. "You're lying."

"No, Grayson told me that." I studied her face but she'd masked her features with a calm expression. Was she trying to mislead me? Someone was. Grayson or Megan? I gave her a quick up and down assessment, but I couldn't tell. "I'm sorry, Megan, but he did deny it."

"You must have misunderstood him. I can see that you get confused easily. And I'm very busy right now. I really don't have time for this." She went off on a long *bragologue* about how hard she worked, much harder than Emery.

While the accountant was talking herself up, I mentally replayed my conversation with Hailey, who'd told me about Megan's snide little comments and put-downs. I wondered if Megan was the insecure one after all and if she was jealous of Emery. Friendships can be complicated. But did their history and ensuing partnership have anything to do with Emery's death? Or the money missing from Emery's clients' accounts?

Did Megan find out about the embezzlement and decide to eliminate possible liability by *offing* her partner? Or did Megan skim the money herself, then make it appear as if Emery was the thief? Not only for the cash, but to hurt Emery or Emery's business and take away her boyfriend? Cash alone is a huge motive, though. Maybe Megan needed extra funds, like, to pay back taxes. Is Megan the other tax payer DiNardo is investigating? Love is the other *biggee* in the motive department. Maybe she did want to get rid of Emery so she could have her boyfriend.

My attention returned to the woman across from me. Her words had wound down, so I asked, "Can you tell me anything about Emery's clients?"

"No, of course not," she insisted. "Confidentiality."

"All right. Thanks for answering my questions." With nothing more to be gained, I rose from the chair.

"I hope I've eased your troubled mind." She showed me to the waiting room and I left through the outer door.

As I walked the hall toward the front stairwell, I passed a fireproof door, so I stopped and shouldered the door open. Crime scene tape blocked the steps going down. I retreated back to the hall and closed the stairwell door after me. Those were the stairs where Clark had met her death. How had the killer lured Clark to this spot? Maybe he didn't have to. It's possible they descended the steps at the same time or met each other as one was coming up and the other going down. Was her death a spur of the moment act of rage on the part of the killer? Or was it planned in advance?

It would've been easy for Megan since she was right on site after all.

I continued down the length of the hall and departed by way of the front stairway. Once home, I fed Boss who was as happy to see me as I was to see him. Giving him a final pat on the head and rub under the chin, I walked out the door into a stiff breeze. Since it was time to monitor the towaway zones, I drove over to Main Street and stationed my self-loader in the alley behind the coffee shop, but the loading zones were all clear. No unauthorized cars. No one cruising around looking for a parking spot. No one even entered the alley.

After a half hour I was bored already, so I called Tanner for a video chat. "Is there anything new?" I asked him right away.

His worried face filled the screen. "The police confiscated my laptop. They also took my phone, but they returned it after a couple hours." So, the sheriff's office was still focusing on Tanner.

"Did they have a search warrant?" My attorney stepdad would've made the sheriff produce a warrant.

"Yeah," he said with a heaviness in his voice. "Did you get a chance to talk to Hailey?"

"I did. She said Megan exercised some control over Emery. The two women's friendship went back years and was complicated."

"Okay." He scrunched his brow in concentration.

"And Hailey thinks Megan's the killer." I looked into the phone screen for Tanner's reaction. Would he agree?

His eyes went wide. "She does?"

"Yes. Hailey said she was friends with those two in college, so she knew them well at that time."

"Hmmm. I'd never have guessed those three were friends. You don't suspect Hailey, do you?" he asked.

"Hailey has an alibi," I explained. "She was in Denver with business associates. That's easy enough to verify. As for Megan, she claimed Grayson was her alibi, but Grayson denied it."

Tanner whistled. "Someone's not telling the truth. That's highly suspicious. But, why does Hailey think Megan did it? What's Megan's motive?"

I explained my theory: jealousy, money, love. Megan had plenty of motives. I knocked my knuckles against my skull and chuckled. "But Megan is probably too obvious. I'm sure the sheriff has thoroughly investigated her."

His face brightened anyway. "Still, it's good work, Laney. Go on."

"Let's see." I read down my suspect list to myself.

"I wish I had all the data on her clients."

"How many have you talked to?"

I ticked the names off. "Nancy Abington who owns the car dealership, Noel Yarborough who runs the wine tasting room, Mike Horn at Main Street Coffee, and Anne Sullivan who has the flower shop. Noel and Mike were each alone Monday night, but the others claim to have alibis. Like, Nancy Abington, who was working that night." I'd done a pretty good job of talking to almost everybody in my lineup. Except one. "There's someone I haven't talked to yet, Lena Fields."

"That makes five suspects." Tanner's eyebrows drew together and he moved his face closer to the camera. "I know some of them, but who's Anne again?"

"Anne's the flower shop lady. Supposedly she was with her husband and grandbaby, but she admits she discovered money missing from her account, so she had a motive, although she claims she only figured it out after Emery died."

"How about Lena? Who's she?"

"Lena works at the sporting goods store on Main Street. Everyone's with a small business that used Spruce Ridge Accounting."

"Okay. You gathered a lot of names, but Emery had to have more clients than those five, right?"

"Right. Megan won't tell me the names of any others."

"She won't?"

"No, darn it. Something about 'client confidentiality.'" I used finger quotes. "Can you believe it?"

At least that got a chuckle. "So, that's how she's going to play this, then?"

"Right?" I fluttered my lips, making the sound like the air let out of a tire. "What's next, Tanner? Do you think you should hire an attorney to defend you? I can ask Will. He probably should've looked over that search warrant."

"I don't have anything to hide, Laney."

"That doesn't mean you don't need a lawyer." I gave him a *don't be stupid* look through the phone camera.

"Maybe you're right. Maybe I do need one." He nodded. "I'll think on it some more. Is there anything else you found out?"

"Let me see." I ran a finger down my page of notes. "The killer tried to revive Emery."

He reared back from the screen. "That's a pretty big clue."

"Why do say that?"

"Because the killer was remorseful. Maybe he didn't mean to kill her? Was it an accident?"

"Ephraim said Emery was shoved pretty hard. Think about this for a minute. If she was pushed from the top of cement stairs with a lot of force, that's fairly intentional. And what were they doing in the stairwell? Did the killer coerce her there, then chuck her down the stairs?"

"When you say it like that…" Tanner looked like he could throw up.

I asked, "Are you okay?"

"No. I'm sick about it. I just want this behind me."

Well, that made two of us.

I rolled down the driver's side window to catch a breath of fresh cool air, the temperature having lowered with the sun long gone. I said, "I've considered every suspect I know about, Tanner. As far as I can tell, the big arrow points to Megan or Grayson or both." I flashed back to Grayson giving Axle a shove when he caught us at Clark's apartment, but thought better of mentioning it. Tanner would get upset and defensive.

"Or me. There's an arrow aimed at me." His lips formed a straight line and the muscles of his jaw worked.

Air swirled down the back of my neck. The night breeze was chilly enough to make me thankful for my sweater.

Tanner sighed. "I got an email about another Chamber event tomorrow. Want to go?"

"Sure, why not? And think about Will. Let me know if I should contact him."

"All right." He looked dejected.

"Okay, then." I leaned back and knocked my knee against the steering wheel, causing my phone to lose balance and topple out of sight. I yelled, "Tanner? Can you still hear me?"

"Yeah. What'd you do?" His voice came from somewhere near the floor.

"Dropped the phone." I poked my hand down the crack between the seats and felt around.

"I see your shoes. Real cute yellow boots."

The phone must've landed near my feet so I reached down to pat the fitted mat underneath the pedals. "You think they're cute, huh?" I'd changed from my orange gladiator sandals to my practical yellow boots.

"I never saw boots with bows on them before."

"Bows?" My boots didn't have bows, but I'd go along with him. "I special ordered them."

"You're special, all right."

I pictured his flirtatious smile and wished I could see his face. Thankfully we could still hear each other.

"Don't you know girls who drive tow trucks have bows on their boots?" My fingers came up with nothing so I opened the driver's door and backed out of the truck. Bent in half at the waist with my face squished to the floor, I extended my arm under the driver's seat. "Do you see my hand? I still can't find my phone."

"*Uh, hum.*" Ephraim's loud throat-clearing jarred me to a stand.

I twirled around and tugged my tee shirt down. My butt had been sticking out a mile and my tee shirt had slid up exposing the back of my bra. "Ephraim! You scared me!" I should've remembered the sheriff often showed up behind the Main Street businesses at this time of night. Normally I looked forward to him stopping by, but tonight I forgot all about him.

He asked, "Who are you talking to?"

"Tanner. I dropped my phone." I flung my arm toward the inside of my truck.

My boyfriend locked onto me with his brown eyes. "You haven't been talking to Tanner about the investigation, have you?"

Oops. My face and neck warmed and probably shone red. I did go over the list of suspects and alibis I'd discovered on my own, so that was all right, but I told Tanner the killer tried to revive the victim, not a fact I'd turned up myself and probably an important clue the police were keeping from the public.

The sheriff lowered his voice to a harsh whisper. "I can't discuss the investigation with you anymore."

"Ephraim, Tanner needs my help since you consider him a prime suspect."

His brown eyes turned black. "Are you working against me?"

I thought my face couldn't get any hotter but I was wrong. Chastised, I tamped down my irritation. "No, I...I..." I had no idea what to say. Seriously!

"I thought I could trust you." His face was a mask of hurt and his voice angry. Was he mad or disappointed or both? He pivoted on the ball of his foot. His cowboy boots thud heavily as he stomped over to his sheriff's cruiser and wrenched open the door. He turned to look back at me. "Delaney, everything is not as it seems." After he climbed inside, he slammed the door shut.

Flushing with self-reproach, I watched the sheriff's vehicle turn out of the alley.

I leaned back down to swipe my hand under the seat. At last my fingers brushed against my cell phone and I snatched it up. "Tanner, you still there?"

"Yeah." His face on the screen appeared guarded and his voice sounded cautious.

"That was Ephraim."

"I figured." His eyes were averted, not looking into the camera.

"Did you hear us?"

A muscle jumped in his cheek. "No, not really."

"He's not happy that I'm talking to you about the investigation. I shouldn't have mentioned the killer tried to revive Emery. Please don't tell him I told you that." I couldn't remember any other undisclosed details I'd shared other than that one, so maybe I could smooth this over.

"You bet." If he'd had on a flirtatious look before, it was long gone now.

"It's all right then." I put on a lot of bravado. "It's all good."

He said goodbye and I pulled my eyes away from

the screen when it went black.

What exactly did Ephraim mean when he said *all was not how it seemed*?

Chapter 15

Just because Tanner knew about the skimming couldn't make him a serious suspect, so what was *not how it seemed*?

I thought back to Clark's other clients. Was the animal-rights granny a cut-throat killer? Was the wine merchant a mean-spirited assassin? The coffee shop owner a homicidal maniac? The sporting goods store kickboxer fighting fit and dangerous? I snapped back to reality. That all seemed too improbable, but *darn*, I wanted to ask Ephraim if he'd verified the suspects' alibis, and in particular, Megan and Grayson, and now I won't be able to. My boyfriend would refuse to talk to me about the investigation anymore, but would he also refuse to talk to me at all?

I needed to shake off this punch to my gut. After the clock struck nine, I left the alley behind and made my way to Oberly Motors. Traffic was non-existent and I arrived in minutes.

Light poured out from the open third stall in the auto bay. Byron held a paint gun operated by an air compressor. I stood back as diffuse fumes floated in the narrow space. When he lowered the electric tool, I called, "Hello, Old Man."

He beamed a gap-toothed smile. "Oh, hi Delaney. I'm just 'bout done here."

"You're working late."

"The owner of this here Camaro wants the paint job done by tomorrow." He pointed to an older Chevrolet, rear-wheel, the typical drive shaft for a classic sports car. "Watcha' up to?"

I didn't want to alarm the Old Man, but I also sought his opinion and knew he would be disappointed if I didn't tell him, so I filled Byron in on my investigation to date.

Byron said, "So ya' talked to the guy at the wine shop on yer own?"

"Yeah, it was no problem after all." I frowned. "Ephraim's not going to give me the inside scoop anymore. What I don't understand is, why are the police so convinced Tanner is a prime suspect? I think there's more going on than I know about."

Byron got a red rag out from a pocket and wiped his neck and hands, then stuffed the rag back into his coveralls. "Sit yerself down there." He pointed to a metal folding chair, so I lowered myself into it while he pulled over another rickety seat.

"Are you going to tell me or what?" I asked.

With his fingers steepled on his belly, Byron answered, "Well now, ya' know Tanner an' you broke up a while ago."

"Yes, yes. And?" What did this have to do with the murder investigation?

"Well now…"

"You already said that part."

"Well now, Tanner, uh, Tanner started goin' out with that young lady."

"Who?" I guess I was being dense. I needed Byron to spell it out.

His gaze skittered around and he wouldn't look me

in the eye. "Emerald Clark."

"What! Tanner should have told me. That really incriminates him." I sat there fuming, trying not to blow up. "It's not like I care if he dates someone else, so why did he hide it from me?" That wasn't a complete lie. I didn't care, or if I did, it was only a teensy bit. "Wait, I thought Clark was with Grayson Thomas."

"You young people. How can anyone keep straight who's goin' out with who? Seems to change all the time." Byron scratched the top of his balding head. "I suppose Tanner and her weren't datin' anymore and she found herself someone new pretty quick."

"Just wait till I talk to him." I cracked my knuckles like some cartoon bad-guy.

Byron swelled up and his shoulders went rigid. "You want me ta' talk to him, cause I will. I'll give him the what-for. He shouldn't go 'round breaking girls' hearts." A dangerous light glinted in his eyes.

My stomach clenched as I realized my mistake. How could I forget Byron considered himself my father substitute and protector? "No, no." I waved a hand in front of his face. "I'm over Tanner. One-hundred percent over and done." My voice came out strangled and I hoped my words sounded sincere. Cause they were. Absolutely. For real. *Sincerious!* Now I just had to repeat that to myself about a thousand more times.

"Are you sure, Delaney, 'cause I can—"

"—Nah, it's all good. Really." I blushed under his gaze.

His angry-bear-look retreated and his knees snapped as he stood. " Okay, then. If you're sure." His hand snagged my shoulder and gave it a squeeze.

I patted his fingers. "Take care, Old Man."

"You, too, Delaney."

I went out into the inky black night and climbed into my little Italian job. The wail of the Fiat filled the air as I accelerated for home.

When Ephraim said everything was not as it seemed, he was referring to this damning history between Tanner and Emery. Why didn't Ephraim tell me they had dated? Did my boyfriend think I still held feelings for Tanner? He was a sheriff, used to reading people's body language and verbal cues. And I wasn't hard to read with my blushing complexion.

I needed to make things right. I hit Bluetooth and spoke into the phone, "Call Ephraim."

He picked up right away. "Delaney?" Good. He wasn't screening my calls.

"I'm sorry, Ephraim. I should've kept our conversations private."

"I'm sorry, too. I don't really think you're undermining me."

I released a tense breath. "You're right, I'm not. I'm only trying to find out the truth."

"Even if it leads to Tanner?"

"Yes, but honestly, I don't think he could've had anything to do with Clark's death." I didn't, even if they'd dated. Tanner was just not capable.

A moment passed, then Ephraim said, "I understand."

"Do you, really?"

"Yes."

My tight fingers relaxed and my stomach stopped churning. "Are we still on for tomorrow night?"

"Of course. I'll see you then."

"Okay." I tapped the end-call button and pumped the

179

brakes to turn off Fifth onto Pine Street.

Now that I'd had time to consider it, I had to admit the sheriff had reason to suspect Tanner after all, because the police always focused on romantic relationships in a murder investigation. But other than the two of them dating, was there another reason to suspect Tanner?

Did Tanner find out Emery and Grayson had broken up? Did he stalk her at her office and make a play to get her back? Perhaps he begged her to pick up where they left off. She said, no. Tanner grabbed Emery, shook her, and threw her down the stairs. Realizing what he'd done, he gathered her in his arms and tried to give her the kiss of life, but it was too late.

OMG, I could just picture this situation. Like a tragic movie. If I could, the cops would. But Tanner was not, could not, be the man in that scene.

I knew him well, and it was inconceivable that he would do such a thing. Tanner would never have intended to hurt a woman. He respected boundaries. And if he had hurt her accidently, he would've owned up to it right away and called 9-1-1. So, I didn't really want to believe it. But, on the other hand, he'd basically lied to me by not telling me about their relationship. Did he have a dishonest side to him? Could he be guilty? Should I consider the possibility? I was veering wildly back and forth. I always considered Clark's clients as potential suspects, but never Tanner. Had my former boyfriend just become a more viable suspect?

Everything with Tanner was not straightforward as I thought.

Ephraim was right. *All was not how it seemed.*

****

The next morning I texted the *numero uno* suspect—

by that I mean, Tanner—to meet at the Chamber of Commerce event that day. I arrived ten minutes before the session was to start.

Nancy Abington, of Abington Auto Sales, stood in a small group of people I didn't know. Dressed as always in an expensive jacket and skirt, and enviable shoes, she turned her head when the mayor entered the room. Her eyes lit up and she elbowed away from the man standing on her right to get to the mayor. With a full plate of cookies, Anne Sullivan, manager of Sullivan's Flower Shop, struck out from the crowd around the refreshment table toward the other side of the room. Her pink sweatshirt was emblazoned with the message, *Save the Horned Owl*, and a rendering of an owl with its talons out…clutching a bunny? The guy who owned Main Street Coffee, Mike Horn, took Anne's spot at the table and began chatting up the cute teenage girl refilling the coffee urn. I heard Noel Yarborough's voice, the one who ran the wine tasting room. He was swearing about something, so I half-turned where I'd taken a seat, and we exchanged long cold looks.

When a harsh scrape sounded on my left, I turned back around to find Mike Horn sinking onto the folding chair next to me. "Hey, Delaney."

"Nice to see you here, Mike. You weren't at the last meeting." I screeched my seat a few inches away from his.

"I can't come to every event. Once a month is enough, but the Chamber president keeps calling for extra meetings."

"Why? Is there an urgent issue?" I didn't even know. Not being a member, I just showed up occasionally.

"A new parking garage off Main. That's why I came today. This affects my business." He gave me a wink. "It affects you, too. That must be why you're here."

"I didn't know about the garage."

"It'll help traffic congestion and bring in more customers, so I'm all for it. I might even need to hire more baristas."

"Is that why you were talking to that young girl?" My gaze swiveled to the refreshment table and back, and I gave Mike a pointed look.

A smile cracked his lips open. "We were talking about who supplies the coffee for these meetings. But I'll go back and ask if she's looking for a job. Thanks for giving me the idea."

I gave him a narrowed-eyed *don't be a perv* look, but he got up and strode back to the coffee table.

Out of the corner of my vision, I caught Owen Eckerd sitting down heavily in the chair to my right. He was hard to miss in his bright orange jersey and beard.

I jerked my head toward him. "Owen, did you know Emerald Clark, the accountant?"

His eyes pinged around the room. "Why do you think I knew her?"

I said, "You used to monitor her condo parking lot." He gave me a blank look. "You know, Ridgeside Condominiums. She lived there." Owen Eckerd, the owner of the ugly green tow truck, had the Ridgeside Condominium Association towing contract before I did.

"I don't know the residents." Wiping his forehead with the back of his hand, Owen let his sleeve fall back exposing his medical bracelet.

The gavel hit the podium with a sharp crack announcing the meeting was about to start. Just then

Tanner burst through the door. He barely broke stride when he spotted me and nodded, then he seized an empty chair near the front. The president went on to explain that the zoning commissioner had set a hearing for approval of a parking structure one block east of Main Street, and the meeting was open for discussion as to whether the Chamber should take a position.

I was just wondering why anyone would oppose something that sorely needed, when Anne Sullivan raised her hand. "Mr. Chairman, I heard the parking deck will be three stories tall. Do we really want the tallest building in our historical downtown to be a parking deck? And what about an environmental impact study?" I could picture this woman holding a placard, *Save Historic Spruce Ridge*, to go along with her *Save the Horned Owl* sweatshirt.

Her question started off a lively discussion, and there seemed to be equal support for and against the idea.

The President hit the gavel again. "I have a question for one of our members." We all did quick over-the-shoulder glances and gave each other questioning looks. He cleared his throat, drawing everyone's eyes back to the front. "Tanner Utley, what do you think about the parking structure?"

A perceptive line of inquiry. A parking deck would be a positive thing for every other business, but not for the business of hauling illegally parked cars.

Tanner answered, "I think it's a much needed improvement. Convenient parking will bring more customers to Main Street. You want more customers, don't you?"

Everyone's heads started to bob up and down and a low murmur went through the audience. A few more people spoke up in favor of the structure. Tanner had turned the tide, because the decision would be based on money and profits, of course. The president answered more questions, describing how the plans included a generous amount of mature landscaping that would beautify the structure. The idea that the tall building would be an eyesore seemed to be forgotten.

The meeting broke up and several people surrounded Tanner.

I located Anne at the refreshment table and cornered her before she could get away. "I'm glad you're concerned about the environment."

"Thank you." The corners of her mouth twitched up. "At least the parking deck plans include lots of trees."

"Right," I agreed. "I found out Emery's funeral is going to be in Nebraska."

Her trace of a smile fell. "That's disappointing, but thanks for letting me know."

"I suppose there's not a whole lot of funerals in Spruce Ridge," I told her.

"Not until lately." She gave me a suspicious look as if I had something to do with that. "There's someone over there I need to talk to." She waved in a vague direction, then left me standing there alone. I noticed the crowd around Tanner had parted so I made a beeline for him.

"I know the city could use a parking deck," I said, "but what about the towaway zones, Tanner? How's it going to impact the tow away zones? Isn't that a big part of your income?" And mine.

He shrugged an acknowledgement, but said, "There will always be people who park illegally, just not as many. I'd just as soon focus my business elsewhere.

There's always plenty of calls for tows."

He had plenty of calls. Me, not so much. I chewed on my bottom lip.

"Don't worry, you won't even miss that work." Tanner slid his hand down my back and electricity crackled between us.

I took in a sharp breath, painfully aware of his proximity. "I have a beef with you."

Surprise registered on his face. "You're that opposed to the parking deck?"

"No, of course not." I flapped a hand, then gave him a narrow-eyed look. "You never told me you dated Emery."

"Huh?" He raised an eyebrow at me.

"You and Emery went out." I had a pain in my stomach that was probably jealousy if I'd admit it to myself.

He pursed his lips, looking for a moment like he was going to deny it, then thought better of it. "How did you find out?"

"Does it matter? Why didn't you tell me yourself?" I fisted my hands on my hips and glanced around the room, trying to keep from growing agitated.

He ducked his head to catch my eye. "I didn't want to because I still care about you." He studied me with an uncertain look.

I opened my mouth but no words came out. Probably given that my breath had caught in the back of my throat.

A man's voice reached our ears. "That Emerald Clark got what was coming to her."

Tanner and I whipped our heads around. Only a few feet away, Mike Horn and Noel Yarborough were in a close discussion with Nancy Abington. It might have been one of the two men, but which one?

Noel caught us staring. He gave me a *mind-your-own-business* glare before suggesting to the others loud enough for me hear, "Let's go over to my place where we can talk about this. In private."

Mike held the door open for Nancy, then went out with Noel trailing behind. A woman jogged over and yelled, "Wait up. I'm coming, too."

I recognized her as the kickboxer, Lena Fields, from the sporting goods store. Short hair in a boyish cut, pretty face, slim, athletic build, outdoorsy. Her tee shirt read, *Better to fight than to die*. She went through the exit on Noel's heels.

I gripped Tanner's sleeve as I stared after her. "That was Lena."

"Who?"

"One of the suspects." I turned back to Tanner. "Let's go over there. We can act like we agree with whatever it is they're talking about and find out a few things."

He concurred with a stiff nod.

We hustled out the door and took separate cars to Noel's wine tasting room on the corner of Tall Chief Road and Bald Eagle. I parked my humble Fiat beside Tanner's humongous flatbed and unpacked myself from the front seat. Sirens whooped from a couple blocks away, then several city police cruisers swept down Tall Chief Road and disappeared around the bend. Quiet reigned once again on this busy corner, and Tanner and I looked at each other.

He asked, "What's the plan, Laney?"

"I don't have one."

Chapter 16

The overhead doors to the wine tasting room were rolled up all the way giving the place an open-air feel and exposing the group gathered at the bar. Their voices carried over. I said, "Look, the tasting room's open to the public. Let's just join them. It's not like they're having a secret meeting in a back room."

"All right. I can take the lead, Laney."

A woman I didn't know was behind the counter with Noel. Nancy and Mike perched on barstools with wine glasses in front of them. Nursing a bottled water, Lena had propped herself on a stool to Nancy's right.

Their gazes snapped in our direction as we strode inside, but Noel's close-set eyes narrowed at me in particular. "What's the *effing* idea? What are you doing here?" The others looked uncomfortable, shifting in their seats.

Tanner answered, "We know you're discussing Emery. She was my accountant, too, and I'm not happy about how she took care of my books. We figured you felt the same way."

Their angry stares bounced off Tanner.

He stood his ground. "We overheard you talking about Emery. We're not here to accuse anyone of anything. We just want to share information."

"Yeah, yeah, okay." Noel visibly relaxed and everyone else blew a collective sigh of relief. The woman behind the bar grabbed a load of bar towels and headed toward the back.

Tanner trained his eyes on the group until his gaze stopped at Nancy. "So, go ahead, resume what you were saying. Don't let us interrupt."

Nancy spat out the words, "Clark screwed me out of tens of thousands of dollars. The police froze her accounts and I can't get my money back. My operating budget is strained this month. Don't they know I have a business to run?" Everyone bobbed their heads up and down. She lifted her shoulders in a slow shrug. "Of course it's not really the fault of the police. This is Clark's doing."

I studied Lena Fields. "You work at the sporting goods store?"

"I own it. That's my store." She acted insulted, like I had suggested she was only a lowly sales clerk.

"That's right. We're all business owners here." Nancy nudged her wine glass toward Noel. "Could I have a little more?"

"Sure." Noel poured another sample into her glass then pointed a finger between Tanner and me. "Do you two want a tasting? I've got a Garnacha open."

I'd never heard of that. I asked, "A Garnacha?"

"A light red with aromas of blackberries, lower in tannins but with a zing." Noel plucked two glasses off a shelf and filled each with a short pour. He set the glasses in front of us, so Tanner and I hitched ourselves up on two empty stools. It was still early in the afternoon, but who cared?

Nancy continued *dissing* Clark along the same vein, and the others chimed in, too, while Tanner and I remained quiet, listening. So...no getting around it,

Clark's clients did have anger going and, yes, their alibis should definitely be doublechecked.

I kicked my heels against the stool rung and leaned one elbow on the bar. "Nancy, when I asked you earlier if you knew of any motives Emery's clients might have, you said you didn't."

She moved her head side to side. "When did I say that?"

"When I brought you a caramel macchiato and we talked about repo work."

Nancy said, "Well, what I said is still true." Her eyes cut to Mike, then over to Noel. "At least for this group. None of us killed her, not over the money she owes us. We're not here to talk about that. We're here to figure out how to get our money back."

"I know you have an alibi, Nancy, but are you aware that neither Mike nor Noel have alibis?" My eyes shot between the two men. "Mike was alone at home, and Noel was working here by himself, but doesn't have the names of any customers to confirm it."

Mike piped up, "Emery didn't steal from me. I didn't lose any money. So, I don't have a motive. And if I don't have a motive, I don't really need an alibi."

"Why are you here, then?" I asked.

Noel sneered. "Why are you here? What about you?"

I crossed my arms and leaned my elbows on the counter. "What about me? What do you want to know? Ask away."

"Did you kill her?" Noel leaned in with an eager look.

"That's a hard no. I was with my roommate Axle that night, and besides, I have no motive. Clark didn't

189

skim my account, either." Ha. I had nothing to skim. Lucky me.

Tanner's smile was stiff. "And as for my alibi, I was working that night, just like the two of you." His chin bobbed toward Mike and Noel, then he looked past the others to Lena. "Do you have an alibi? You're pretty quiet over there."

Lena huffed out a breath, outraged. "I was teaching a self-defense class." She shot off her stool, her posture shouting anger. "You want to make something of that?"

"Whoa, whoa, I was just asking." Tanner raised his palms as if to ward her off. "We're on a fact-finding mission here, that's all."

Defiance and anger lit her eyes, but she popped back onto her stool. The others cast nervous glances at each other. I was itching to get out my notepad so I could make notes.

Nancy tossed down one last swallow of wine. "Thanks, Noel, but I'm leaving. This discussion is not helping anything. I'll see you all later." She pushed herself off her stool and straightened her skirt. She looked at me directly. "Bye, Delaney."

"Bye."

Lena said, "I'm outta here, too. I have a class tonight." She pinned Tanner and me with a look like *don't try to follow me*. As if we would want to. Then she barreled out the open garage door like an elk on a rampage, with Nancy on her tail.

I gave Tanner a helpless shrug and his shoulders sagged back at me.

"I'll take a bottle of this wine, Noel," I told him. I was more of a beer drinker, but I liked the Garnacha a lot. Noel retrieved a new bottle and poked it into a narrow sack. I gave him my debit card. He swiped my plastic and gave it back to me. Mike remained at the bar with Noel after Tanner and I walked outside.

We halted at Tanner's truck bed. I asked, "What do you think?"

"Lena Fields has an attitude."

"Hostile." I held the bag with the wine bottle in the crook of my arm.

"They all seem upset about the embezzlement."

"Especially Nancy. Thousands of dollars, she said. Tens of thousands." I gave him a wide-eyed look.

"Yeah, that's a lot. I didn't lose that much." Tanner extracted his keys. "I need to head out."

"Okay. Talk again soon?"

He nodded, then climbed inside and fired up his truck. I crammed myself behind the wheel of my Fiat and set the bottle of wine on the passenger's seat. Exiting the parking lot, we went our separate ways.

Unspoken between us were Tanner's words that he still cared for me. I didn't know what to make of that, so I took a moment to consider it. What was going on between us? I hoped, nothing. No really. Ephraim and I are together now. Then I considered that thought for a long moment.

I drove over to Roasters on the Ridge to get my caffeine-high on. The wine had made me sleepy, even though I'd only had a short sample. I parked in back and caught Axle clomping down the apartment stairs. His slouchy jeans were riding low and his Indie band tee shirt was looking a little washed out. I got out and we approached each other.

"Whassup?" Axle bumped my fist.

I said, "I don't know where to begin." We entered

the coffee shop together and stepped in line. I breathed in the warm combination of coffee, cinnamon, and nutmeg. "Why aren't you at work, cuz'?" I followed Axle as he inched up the line.

"Byron said I didn't need to go in until two today. I'm heading over in a few minutes."

Axle often got a ride from a buddy, but I asked, "You want a lift?"

"Sure. Thanks, Delaney." He told the barista, Guy, "Caramel latte, please."

I ordered, "Double shot."

When we were waiting at the other end of the counter, Axle elbowed me. "Look over there." He jerked his head like he was having a spasm.

I twirled around to see what he was trying to tell me. Megan and Grayson sat at the corner table, their heads together as if in an intimate conversation. Megan grabbed a phone off the table and Grayson told her to give it back. She giggled and he prodded his shoulder against hers. I had a tinge of jealousy at their flirty relationship, not sure Ephraim and I ever looked like that.

Guy called out our names and Axle and I shuffled over to pick up our drinks. After we got cardboard sleeves from the condiment cart, it was too late to talk to the couple. They'd left the coffee shop.

Kristen came out from her office. "I have time for a break if you do."

I gave Axle a questioning look and he nodded. The three of us sat down at an empty table and I sipped my coffee through the to-go lid, scalding my tongue.

"What's new?" Kristen wanted to know.

I brought my friends up to speed on my investigation

and what went down at the wine shop. Axle was more interested in the city's new parking deck than the new suspect—Lena— and Kristen just shook her head at the lack of alibis. Nancy Abington, Anne Sullivan, and Lena Fields claimed to have alibis—as yet unconfirmed— Mike Horn and Noel Yarborough did not. And Tanner, of course, didn't either.

I told them, "The flower shop lady had a picture of herself with her husband and grandbaby to prove her alibi, but I don't know when the photo was taken. Nancy claimed to be at the auto dealership." I tapped the edge of my drink with my thumb. "Hailey at Friendly Finance gave me an alibi, too, but I haven't checked it out yet. She knew the victim, so I guess that might make her a suspect, however unlikely."

Kristen clucked her tongue. "Ask Ephraim. I'm sure he's talked to all the witnesses."

I scrunched my nose. "I don't know. Ephraim's being touchy about the investigation."

Axle said, "Use your superpowers, Super Sleuth. You don't need the sheriff."

I cradled my hot drink between my fingers. "Really?"

"Come on, throw that whip around. You can figure this out on your own." Axle gave me a thumbs up.

Kristen said in a teasing tone, "You two are nuts."

"You ready?" Axle pointed his shoes toward the door.

"Yup."

We said goodbye to Kristen, and she slipped back behind the counter. Once out the door, I spied a Honda HR-V, front-wheel drive with government plates, parked next to my Fiat. Probably DiNardo's car since he was on the other side of the lot talking to that Owen Eckerd.

"Oh, shit." I shielded my face with one hand and dashed toward my car. "Come on, Axle, hurry up."

Axle dove in the passenger seat and I jumped in the driver's side.

Before I got the engine cranked, DiNerdo was at my window. "Miss Morran." He adjusted his latest bowtie. Pink striped. "One more day," he warned.

"I know already." I shoved the gear in reverse, causing my Fiat to jet backwards, then we sped out of the lot.

Axle smacked me in the arm. "Man, what's his problem?"

I rubbed my elbow. "You know."

"What?"

"He's still after me for the $1,437 I owe per tax code §2.3 something." I rolled my eyes.

He gaped at me. "You haven't paid that yet?"

"You would think so, but no. I got a voice mail that my laptop's fixed, so I thought I'd pick it up first, and try to oppose the assessment." I was going to give that plan one more effort.

"Good luck with that." Axle sighed. "And slow down if you don't want a ticket."

"*Shaaaadup!* How many tickets have you had?"

"Put a cork in it, Delaney."

After dropping off Axle at Oberly Motors, I sat in my tow truck and consulted my notes. It would only take a few moments to check some alibis before heading to the mall for my laptop. The restaurant where Hailey ate dinner at the time of the murder was probably the easiest to confirm, so I called there. The person who answered the phone remembered the dinner meeting because

Friendly's stockholders reserved one of the private dining areas every month.

She even remembered Hailey after I'd described her. She said, "Of course no one can forget Hailey. She's pretty and she's nice, too."

I wrote a note on my list that Hailey's alibi was confirmed like I knew it would be. I was contemplating which alibi to check next when my cellphone rang.

The name popped up on caller ID: Patrick Crump, the repo agent with Abington Auto Store. I answered, "Hello, Patrick. How are you?"

He said by way of greeting, "I need you to recover the Hyundai Elantra again."

"Clyde Dankworth's?" I gasped.

"Yes, that's the one."

"What do you mean? I already delivered that to Abington's." In fact, I was waiting for my repo money to be paid at the end of the month.

"I know, but Nancy let him have it back when he wrote her a check to catch up on the payments. And guess what? The check bounced."

Laughing, I slapped the steering wheel. "Stop. You're killing me. Why would Nancy accept a check from him?"

Crump let out a whoosh of breath that I could hear over the phone. Then he continued in a low voice, "He's got such an honest face. Even I felt sorry for the guy. But he's one slippery dude."

"Tell me something I don't already know." I recalled Clyde's baby face with his chipped tooth. He looked like an innocent child, despite his thinning hair and attempt at a beard. And he'd tricked me into taking him to Abington's when I delivered the Elantra the first time. Then he'd made off with his car.

Crump said a few words to somebody else that I couldn't make out, then to me, "Clyde's here with me at Ridgeside Condominiums. We're waiting together for you." I understood. Crump wasn't about to leave the man with his car only to disappear one more time.

"On my way."

In jeans with an untucked dress shirt and tie, Patrick leaned against the car alongside Clyde, whose thin arms were crossed over his narrow chest. Clyde gazed into the distance like a kid in a daydream, but I wasn't going to let him fool me again, either.

After I had the Elantra's front end lifted on the back of my self-loader, I told Crump, "I'll let you know once it's delivered to Abington's."

"Good." The repo man extracted his car keys from a pocket and climbed into his gray Ford Taurus, front-wheel drive.

Under Clyde's scrutiny, I secured the straps around the Elantra's wheels, blushing as red as my crimson suede heels, but now was not the time to let that sympathy gene of mine kick in.

But…before I climbed into my truck, I stopped and drummed my lips. Then I told Clyde, "I know someone who might be able to get you another car loan if you need new wheels. It's where I have the loan for my own car."

He smiled. "Really? You'd do that for me?"

I'm a sucker, but keep that on the down low. "Do you want to meet me at Friendly Finance in about a half hour?"

"Sure, Delaney. That'd be great."

"Wait for me there."

"I will. Hey, Delaney, I got a tip for you. There's

going to be a party here tonight and lots of nonresident cars will be parked in the lot."

"How do you know this?"

"There's a flyer in the laundry room. It's an underground party like a rave. Last time the lot was full and my girlfriend complained she couldn't get a parking spot. She had to park three blocks over and make several trips to get her groceries unloaded. It was a pain."

"They still have those kind of parties?"

"Sure, sure."

"Okay. Thanks for the tip." I took off, studying him in my rearview mirror. He ripped a new phone out of a pocket and turned his back to me, no doubt calling for a ride to Friendly. Here's hoping he wasn't calling for a ride to Abington's.

After circling around the back of the dealership lot, I reversed the Elantra into an empty spot outside the quick lube garage. The truck gave an almost imperceptible sway, emitting several moans and tings, and the front of the car lowered to the ground. I retrieved my wheel straps from the Elantra and stowed them under the truck bed.

I swung a sharp look in every direction, like an eagle spying out a snake, but did not see Clyde anywhere. It would be better for everyone if a buddy had driven him over to Friendly Finance to apply for a fresh, new loan, rather than here to steal back his repo'ed Hyundai Elantra.

Just to be safe, I went inside and asked the receptionist to let Patrick Crump know the vehicle had been delivered and if someone could keep an eye on it. And that it might be a good idea to move it inside. The blonde receptionist typed on her computer keyboard, then explained to me, "I sent Patrick your message. He just now got back to the dealership himself."

"We both had to work hard for this repo." I laughed. She laughed in return, obviously good-natured and approachable, necessary qualities when in sales. I asked, "Did you know Emerald Clark, the accountant?"

Her hand went to her throat. "The one murdered?"

"That's the one."

"No, but I heard what happened to her."

"She did the books for the dealership. And Nanc' told me," I said, like good ole' Nancy and I were close friends, "And Nanc' told me…she was working here the night Clark was killed. It's a good thing she has an alibi."

The blonde arched her eyebrows. "You're the one who brings her those lattes from Roasters? What a nice friend."

She believed my stretch of the truth and I went along with it. "We're tight like this." I held out two crossed fingers. "I know her favorite coffee drink is a caramel macchiato." I actually did know her favorite drink. "So, were you working here that night, too?"

"We always work late on Mondays." She scratched her scalp with the end of a pen, then swiveled back to her computer screen as if to look something up. "Let's see…oh yeah, I remember that night. Nancy was here until about five, then she left. I know she was back by six-thirty because one of the sales staff needed her approval on a deal for a new Jeep Gladiator. Those normally sell for forty-seven and he wanted to lower the price to forty-five."

"Forty-five thousand?" I gulped. Wait, I was getting distracted here. "Well, Nanc' did tell me she left to get something to eat." I was such a good liar.

"Yes. She normally takes off for dinner at five and returns by six or six-thirty, then she's here until closing at nine."

"She was definitely gone for an hour?"

"Or an hour and a half. But you and I know she had nothing to do with that woman's death."

"As if!"

We both laughed at the ridiculousness of the idea.

"Yeah, that'd be something for the weird files." She was practically falling out of her chair laughing.

"Oh, *puhleeze*. Get real." I feigned indignation. I told my new confidant, "So long for now," and sauntered out the door.

But back in my truck, I double underlined ole' Nanc's name, scribbled down an hour and a half window of time that constituted the lack of alibi, and surrounded the words with stars.

Chapter 17

Since the mall was on the way to Friendly Finance, I slowed and took a right into the parking lot. No, I'm not here to buy shoes. Although I did a quick pass through the discount shoe store on my way to the laptop repair place, but that only took an extra few seconds. Yeah, deal with it.

The tech guy went to the backroom to find my laptop and brought it out a few minutes later.

He said, "So, the email with the virus attached was from *Tow Trick News*, not *Tow Truck News*. I traced the IP address of the original email sender and it was rerouted offshore. I blocked that address on your computer, but you know these scammers just use a different one the next time, so be careful. Never open an attachment if you don't know who it's from."

I said, "Well, *Tow Trick News* looks a lot like *Tow Truck News*," but I secretly scolded myself.

"Yeah, that's how they do it." He added, "That'll be ninety-five dollars."

This was a hit to my account, and the money might've been better spent paying down my IRS debt, but I couldn't operate my business without my laptop, so there was nothing I could do about it. He ran my debit card through his card reader, then stared at the screen.

"What?" I asked.

"Your card's declined."

"What!" Heat crept up my neck. I brought out my phone and opened my bank app. The balance showed zero. But I hadn't spent the money from my last tow job. I didn't buy those shoes I tried on at the discount shoe store. I knew for a fact that I had a hundred and twenty in that account. I practically shouted, "My bank account's been hacked! How is this possible?" I slammed down a fist on the counter.

The computer tech took a step back, giving me a wide berth. "Jeez, to be cyber attacked twice in a row. That's really bad juju."

"Yeah, what's the chance of that?" My voice was shrill and I needed to dial it back. "Sorry. I guess I'd better call the bank."

"You should do that." He slid my laptop off the counter and stowed it underneath the shelf.

I sprinted to my tow truck and sped out of the lot, the back tires squealing when I took the curve fast, leaving a cloud of dust in my wake. After negotiating the bend at breakneck speed, I was pulled over by a Spruce Ridge officer.

"Delaney, do you know how fast you were going?" the officer asked through my window.

"No, but here are my registration and insurance." I handed him the papers from my glove compartment. I recognized him. Officer York, who worked with Kristen's boyfriend, Zach. I fished my license out of my wallet and gave it to him, as well.

"Twenty over. I'm going to have to write you a ticket." He had on a smug look and took his sweet time over his electronic tablet. "I'm sending you this by email. Are you going to be able to access your messages? I heard about your computer trouble."

"You're just *hahahilarious*." I'd have to tell Zach to quit talking about me. People share information about trouble quickly in a small town. York passed back my license and paperwork and told me to have a nice day.

A speeding ticket was the last thing I needed today. Or ever.

After driving slowly, I parked in the finance company lot. I clambered out from behind the wheel, pushing loose strands of hair back from my face and taking a deep breath.

Clyde was at the front door. "Hope you didn't wait long," I told him.

"Nah, I just got here. Thanks for doing this for me. I really need to get another car. I'm so glad you're here to help me." He gave me a sad smile. "I'm not sure they'll give me a loan, though." My day wasn't going great either, so I understood that hopeless feeling.

I said, "We'll see," and opened the door for both of us. I greeted Hailey, then explained the situation about Clyde's repo, no sugar-coating. "Can Clyde get another car loan so he's not left without transportation? If he gets preapproval, that'll help him find a vehicle in his budget. One that he can afford." I was thinking of my used Fiat.

Hailey gave him a sweep with her eyes. "What are your date of birth and social?"

He rattled off the numbers while Hailey entered them into her computer. Her eyebrows squished together and she pursed her lips. "Mr. Dankworth, your last loan wasn't your first default. It was the second loan in default, and in fact, you didn't make even one payment on either loan. I'm afraid I can't help you."

I tried to maintain my composure but tears gathered in the back of my throat. Not for Clyde! For me! Were cyber thieves out there right now spending the hundred and twenty bucks from my bank account? Was that speeding ticket landing in my mailbox at this moment?

Hailey continued with, "You are a serial loan defaulter. You're causing finance companies like mine to lose thousands of dollars per year." We both stared at the child-man.

I said, "That's pretty lame, Clyde." This reminded me of my social work days. Most of the time the people I tried to help had legitimate needs, but sometimes they didn't.

Clyde raised both palms up in the universal sign of surrender. "Sorry."

"How often does this happen, Hailey?" I asked.

"It helps that we can report these scammers to credit bureaus like this one." She pointed toward the computer screen.

Clyde is a scammer. It goes to show that people are not what they seem. And there are some bad people out there who rip others off. Just like the crooks who sent my computer a virus and withdrew money from my bank account. And the darn police who nabbed me in a speed trap. I choked back a sob.

"Gosh, you really care." Clyde patted my hand. "Thanks for trying, Delaney."

I swiped a tear and rose to a stand. "Thanks, Hailey. I appreciate your time."

I recalled Tanner's words when he explained repo work to me at the very beginning. I'd complained that I felt bad for those folks going through a hard time, that it could be *me* having trouble making *my* car payments. But he'd said there were buyers who didn't even make the first payment and he was right. Clyde Dankworth was one of them. When he didn't pay for the vehicle, that was stealing, not buying. Repo basically means I'm recovering a stolen vehicle for the lienholder. And, if I didn't do the work, someone else would. Like Owen Eckerd with his ugly green truck.

This wasn't personal. This was business, but I often let it get personal.

Note to self: You help others best by doing your job well.

Clyde strolled out of the finance office in front of me. Curious about Owen getting repo work that should be coming to me, I asked the serial repo expert, "Clyde, has a vehicle of yours ever been repo'ed by a guy driving a green tow truck?"

"I know who you mean, Owen."

"You know him?"

He gave me a sideways glance. "Not really. But I've seen his truck around Ridgeside Condos."

"That makes sense because he had the contract to monitor that lot before I did." I had yet to tow one car from the lot. Maybe I wasn't doing a very good job and it would be my turn to lose the contract. I asked, "You knew Emerald Clark, right? She lived there."

"Oh, sure." Clyde took a step off the curb. "And, you know that other tow truck driver? Tanner Utley?"

"Yes." I wondered where he was going with this.

"Tanner was at her apartment all the time."

He kept walking, so I threw out an arm to stop him. "Wait. You're going to have to explain that." Tanner would've been at her apartment since they dated, but the fact still made a bitter taste creep up my throat.

"What can I say? My girlfriend lives a few doors down from Emery's apartment. We saw them together on the balcony." Clyde shook my hand away. "There's my girlfriend now." He trotted over to a Kia Rio, front-wheel drive, with an attractive young woman at the wheel. What was she doing with a loser like Clyde?

Curious, but the next puzzle to solve was not about Clyde, but about what happened to my bank account.

Once in my truck, I phoned the bank. The help desk answered and I said, "I think I've been hacked."

The man on the other end calmly asked me for my name and account number and verified my identity. He confirmed my account was at zero balance. He said, "Your funds haven't been accessed illegally. The IRS made a withdrawal and depleted your balance."

"They can't do that." I flopped back against the car seat stunned, but hadn't Will mentioned something about levies and drastic measures?

"Yes they can, unfortunately. Is there anything else I can help you with?"

"Uh, no, I guess not."

"Have a nice day." There was a click and the line went dead.

I stared at my phone for a moment, then fished DiNardo's card out from the bottom of my purse and dialed his number. When he answered, I exploded into the speaker, "This is Delaney and I need to talk to you."

"Good afternoon, Ms. Morran."

"Yeah, well, I just found out the IRS took all my money from my bank account and I want it back."

"That's not how it works. But I'm glad you called because I agree we do need to talk."

"Why didn't you warn me when I saw you earlier today?"

"You knew about the deadline."

"You told me the deadline is tomorrow."

"We noticed your account getting dangerously low and took what funds were available before there was nothing to take. As it is, there wasn't enough money in your account to bring your balance current. You now owe $1,284.36 per tax code §2.3104.141a."

I stabbed the phone to hang up on him. I was about to launch my phone out the truck window, but instead tried to concentrate on breathing. Inhale. Exhale. Inhale. Exhale. I considered phoning my mother, thinking what I would say, as I took a last bracing breath.

"Mom, I hate to ask, but I need a loan. Fourteen hundred dollars." Enough to pay the IRS. Enough to pay the computer repairman.

"Of course, Laney. And you don't have to pay me back until you're firmly on your feet and able to support yourself." Did ya' catch that? In case you didn't, that was an insult. "And, Laney, you could always move back home and save expenses."

Not just no, but hell no. I put the back of my hand to my forehead wishing to be anywhere else but on a phone call such as this.

And that's why I decided against calling Mother. I just knew the conversation would go the way I imagined it. My mother loved me with all her heart, and I loved her back, but we couldn't live together. Something not to be contemplated. Move on.

Note to self: never, ever mess with the IRS again. Did I say never, ever? I meant never, ever, ever, ever.

I'd been short on funds before and relied on credit cards to get me through a rough patch. After that I'd cut up all my plastic except for my debit card, which I used as a credit card, but only to withdraw out of my bank account. So, no falling back on credit this time. I needed to figure out something else or Mom might just get her wish.

Ugh. Cue the music. A tear escaped and rolled down my cheek.

Buck up. Everything was going to work out, I told myself.

Several insurance companies owed me money for clearing the highway during that big pile-up, but who knew when I would see that cash. I was scheduled to monitor the Main Street no-parking zones tomorrow and again Thursday, and the ongoing weeks after that—at least until the parking deck went in—but there was no certainty of making money every night. I might not catch anyone parking illegally. Abington Motors owed me for the repo of Clyde Dankworth's Hyundai Elantra. Only, Abington paid for their repos at the end of the month which was still weeks away.

But the repo check was my best bet for immediate money. Nancy Abington had complained about being short on operating cash herself, so she'd understand if I asked for the repo check early. She might appreciate my need, but she might not be able to pay me. It was still worth a try. The worst she could say is no.

The chatty receptionist waved me back to her office when I arrived with a caramel macchiato for my good friend, Nanc. I bustled down the hall between the sales cubicles and landed the hot drink on Nancy's desk before taking a seat.

"You're spoiling me," Nancy gushed as she picked up the drink I'd snagged from Roasters for free.

"I have a favor to ask," I admitted. "Could you please cut my repo check early? I need the money to pay the balance I owe the IRS and the deadline is tomorrow."

"Certainly." She didn't hesitate and I breathed a sigh of relief. She lifted her phone and said, "Connect me to bookkeeping." Then she instructed a subordinate to cut the check. After she hung up Nancy said, "Just ask the receptionist on the way out and she'll run back and get the check."

"Thanks so much. You don't know how this helps me out. While I'm here…" I paused. This could be a big mistake, but I clenched my purse in front of me and said, "…there's something I need cleared up. You know how we were all at the wine tasting room talking about alibis?"

"Yes?" Her gaze held a question.

"Well…I found out you left the dealership to eat dinner the night Clark was killed."

She looked around as if trying to figure out what I was asking. "Oh, you think I might've had time to run over to Clark's office and do the deed." She chuckled. "I went out to eat with our top salesman. You can check with him, Vance Jones."

My muscles eased. "Thanks again for being so helpful."

"Are you making progress in the investigation?"

"Not really. You probably know the suspects better than I do. I mean, you recognized them at the police station and you knew their names."

"We're all acquainted from the Chamber of Commerce. You should join, too."

"I think you're right. Well, I won't take any more of your time." I leaned across her desk and shook her hand, certain her alibi would be confirmed. And on the way out, I stopped at the cubical with Vance Jones' nameplate on the partition, and he corroborated her story.

By the time I got to the lobby, the friendly receptionist had my check ready for me. Once at my truck, I jumped up and down in my red suede heels and screamed into my hand, "Yes, yes, thank you." Then I fanned myself with the check. Then I kissed it and tucked it into my purse.

Since it was after bank hours, I drove over to the nearest ATM to deposit the money. But after the machine sucked the check into the slot, a message came on the screen that the funds were not immediately available due to the bank's hold policy. Well, I could show up at the bank in the morning for the cash. It wasn't enough money to pay DiNerdo in full, but maybe he would take a hefty partial payment.

It was with a lighter heart that I prepared for my date with Ephraim. I dressed in my high-rise jeans, a pale green top, and green plastic flip-flops embellished with daisies, and opened the bottle of wine I'd bought at Noel Yarborough's tasting room, the Garnacha. Pork chops, kale, and an avocado sat on my counter ready to try in a new recipe. I went ahead and sampled one glass of wine and put on soft country music. I chopped the kale, a lemon, snap peas, and the avocado and made a bed of the fresh vegetables on two plates like they do on those cooking shows.

Ephraim knocked on the door and came inside with a bunch of fresh daisies. My favorites. They matched my shoes. I poured him a glass of wine and stuffed the daises in a jug of water. While he settled on a stool at the counter, I splashed a little olive oil in the bottom of my cast iron skillet and rested the skillet on a stovetop burner. I breaded the pork chops, and Ephraim sipped his wine.

I laughed in what I thought was a flirtatious way and tried to bat my eyelashes. "I know you don't want to talk about the investigation anymore, but I can't help myself. I'd really like to know if everyone's alibis checked out."

He chuckled. "It's all right, Delaney. No need to wheedle it out of me, just ask. If I can tell you, I will. Just don't ask me about Tanner. You know I can't talk about him."

"Right." The number one suspect. I didn't really want to talk about my ex-boyfriend either.

The sheriff asked, "Whose alibis?"

"Anne Sullivan at the flower shop for one. I know you brought her in for questioning. She said she was babysitting her grandbaby at the time Clark was killed, but was she?" I lifted a breaded chop with the tongs and placed it in the sizzling skillet.

He sprang up to help me at the stove, and we stood next to each other watching the chop brown in the pan. He asked, "When did you talk to her?"

"I went in to buy a plant."

"You just happened to go into *her* flower shop to buy a plant?"

I felt his eyes on me. "Yes, I did. About her alibi?" I prompted, hoping to get him to spill all.

He had his tongue against his teeth, like he was about to *tsssk,* but instead said, "All right, I'll tell you so you don't go bothering her again. I talked to her husband and her daughter. They confirmed Anne was babysitting that night."

I mentally crossed her off the list. "What about Noel Yarborough?"

"You've been pestering him, too? Well, you can

quit. He was at the wine tasting room during the time period in question. A sheriff's cruiser was out on Tall Chief Drive at five and again at five-thirty and noted Yarborough inside with a customer. You can see clearly through those large garage doors he leaves open."

"What a coincidence. Lucky for Noel." I crossed him off my mental list, too.

"Well, there's been a series of crimes out that way, so there was a police presence in the area."

"How about Lena Fields?" I gave the sheriff a sideways glance.

"Fields was holding a kickboxing class at six that night."

"Is kickboxing like martial arts?"

"Yeah, and you might think about taking a class for self-defense yourself, the way you stir up trouble."

"Maybe I will." I nestled the second breaded chop in the skillet next to the first one. Then I twisted toward Ephraim. "Wasn't Clark on her way to a self-defense class when she was murdered?"

"Good memory, Delaney. Yes, she was."

"Lena's class?"

"Yes. But Clark didn't make it."

"Right." I turned back to the sizzling pan. "I was able to verify Nancy's and Hailey's alibis myself. Nancy was out to dinner with her top salesman, and Hailey was also at a restaurant, one in Denver. And as far as Mike Horn goes, he told me Clark didn't skim his account, so he doesn't have a motive."

His black eyebrows hovered near his dark hairline. "You've been busy. I hope none of these people are upset that you questioned them."

"Those last three are friends of mine, sort-of friends.

They're not concerned." At least I didn't think so. "And as far as the other suspects, Megan said she was with Grayson, but Grayson denied that he was with her. Did you get the truth out of them?"

"I was able to pin their alibis down." Ephraim nodded, but his attention was drawn to the skillet as he shook salt, then pepper, over the chops. "Grayson did stop at Megan's apartment later that night, but not at the time of Clark's death. It doesn't matter since they have other verified alibis. When the victim was killed, Megan was shopping at the mall. A clerk remembers her, plus she had a time-stamped receipt. There are witnesses who will testify that Grayson was at his office."

I shoved a hand on my waist and waved the tongs around with the other hand. "Humph! Why didn't they just tell me that?" My voice rose in a crescendo.

"Because you're not with the sheriff's department." His voice had gone up, too, but in a teasing way, and he laughed.

"There's that," I admitted. "So, I assume the killer didn't leave fingerprints?"

"None that we found. There were too many in the office to be relevant and the doorknob to the stairwell was wiped clean." Ephraim breathed in the aroma from the chops. "I think the meat's done."

I extracted the pieces and placed one on each of the plates with the vegetables I'd prepared earlier. My boyfriend refreshed our glasses of wine and we took seats at the kitchen table.

I said, "It seems all my suspects are eliminated, then."

"I'll tell you this, Delaney, Tanner has not been eliminated. He's still at the top of the list."

I gave him my best *what-the-hell* glare. "Please tell me you're investigating other suspects? She had more clients than the ones we discussed, right?"

"Hey, don't go looking at me like that. Of course we are questioning everyone. And I have some good news." Ephraim spotted a napkin to his mouth before resuming. "Emerald Clark's files have been returned to her office, including your thumb drive. You're not the only one who needs their files back so they can resume business. By the way, forensics determined Clark didn't even open your drive, so it was never necessary to the investigation. It wasn't even copied to her computer."

Yes! Yes! Yes! I chewed briskly on a piece of kale. I'd pick up my thumb drive tomorrow and prove to DiNerdo once and for all that the IRS is wrong.

I'm tired of DiNerdo's strongarm tactics.

And I can't believe Tanner is still a suspect.

I'm not letting any of this go. Neither the money owed nor the murder.

Chapter 18

After Ephraim left, I watched an old movie with a bowl of buttered popcorn until around eleven, then turned off the set and got up to dress in black jeans, a black sweatshirt, and black chucks. I drove the short distance over to Ridgeside Condominiums and pulled up to the curb on Larkspur Avenue across from the pale yellow apartment building. The comforting smell of my truck...diesel and motor oil and a woodsy scent...was such a contrast with the burnt popcorn aroma I'd left behind at my apartment.

The rave party was in full swing. Several balconies were crammed with laughing people, lights flashed from the windows, and loud music blasted into the cool night air. It looked as if every available spot was taken in the parking lot, and some cars were even wedged in between the dumpsters and on the lawn.

Part of me wanted to join the fun, but I wasn't in my party clothes. I was in all black. And I hadn't needed to dress this way. Nobody was going to notice me in the crowded parking lot with all the pandemonium.

Except somebody did. A Chevrolet Malibu, front-wheel drive, stopped next to me and the window wound down. A woman spoke. "Hey, are you going to tow some of these cars?"

I hunched my shoulders up to my ears and took a deep breath. "I was thinking about it."

"Good. I can't find a parking place. And if the noise doesn't quit by twelve, I'm calling the cops." The window buzzed up and the woman took off. She drove several blocks up the street, then nosed to the curb and got out. She hoofed it back to the complex and entered the lobby of the gray building.

Well, I had an hour, then.

I turned into the lot to start moving cars off the lawn. None of them had the required parking permit, but even if they had, the residents weren't supposed to park on the grass. Within a half hour I'd snatched three vehicles with my self-loader, and another four by the time the clock struck midnight. I'd filled the secure lot I used at Oberly Motor's and was considering calling Tanner to come help fill up his impound lot, when three black and white police cruisers arrived, their yellow light bars flashing on and off the trio of apartment buildings. The woman resident must have made good on her promise to call the Spruce Ridge Police.

The ravers flew out the doors and ran for their cars. It looked like a concert crowd trying to clear out, everyone backing out at once and jamming the exit onto Larkspur. I sat back in my driver's seat to wait, planning to do one more pass to see if any illegal cars remained after everyone else had left.

A fourth black and white drove up beside me and idled the engine. Officer Zach Bowers, Kristen's boyfriend, the cop who always seemed to be Johnny-on-the-spot, climbed out and looked at me over the top of his patrol car. "Hello, Delaney. Did you remove some of vehicles from this lot?"

"I did. Seven. I was just about to call them in, honestly. Do you want the VINs?"

"Sure, send them to the dispatcher before we start to get reports of stolen cars."

I leaned out my window. "So, some party, huh?"

"The last time there was one of these raves we arrested a couple of drug dealers. Maybe we'll catch a few more, if you were lucky enough to tow any of their cars before they could get away." He stared up at the balcony and I looked, too. The strobe lights from inside had shut off and the music had gone silent. Two officers frog-marched a man in ragged jeans and over-sized sneakers out the lobby door and over to a police car.

"Looks like they got one, at least. I suppose you heard I got a speeding ticket?"

"Sorry I can't fix it for you, Delaney."

"I know. See you later, Zach." I ducked my head back into the cab. The lot had emptied and I didn't feel the need to do any more patrolling after all.

Before I was halfway home, I received the first call to pick up one of the vehicles I'd towed. I went straight to the impound lot and waited for the owner to show up. While I sat there, I called the police dispatcher and rattled off all the VINs like I'd promised Zach. All but two of the vehicles were reclaimed when I decided to head home at two.

Since I'd collected all those fees when the drivers came for their vehicles, a bundle of money was filling up that bank account of mine. Thank you for organizing the rave, whoever you are.

Now I had more than enough to pay the IRS. And buy groceries and pay my cell phone bill and take care of my speeding ticket. And maybe get those cute shoes I'd tried on at the discount shoe store. But best of all, I'd pick up my laptop. With my flash drive back, I can quit trying to reconstruct my records, because I'm still going to talk to Will about filing some sort of appeal with the IRS. I'm slaying it!

I pictured throwing the money at Nerd the DiNerdo—right in his face.

N-yeh, n-yeh, n-yeh.

****

The vibrating phone danced on the bedside table, waking me from sleep, all groggy and disoriented. My finger punched the button to answer while I kept my eyes shut. The Spruce Ridge police dispatcher was on the line with a vehicle that needed towed.

"Now?" I opened one eye to look at the clock. Four in the morning. Was it someone else from the rave?

"Normally we wouldn't request a vehicle removal at this time of night, but the owner's been called in to work at the hospital. Her vehicle was vandalized and isn't drivable. It's blocking her driveway out on Tall Chief Drive, and she can't get her second vehicle out of the garage to get to work."

"Okay, on my way." I pulled myself out of bed and picked strands of hair from my mouth. A doctor or nurse needed my help, not a rave partier.

With the Fiat's windows rolled down and the dry scent of pine blowing in, I was able to wake up a little before picking up my tow truck and proceeding south, then west on Tall Chief Drive. This was a winding road that made me feel as if I was out in the country, although it was within city limits. There were a few older houses that must have been on farmland at one time before Spruce Ridge had expanded. I passed through the achromatic scene with homes shuttered for the night and pulled in to the drive of a small ranch with a one stall garage.

A Chrysler Voyager minivan, front-wheel drive, was butted up against the garage door. The halogen light attached to the house buzzed loudly overhead. The Voyager didn't look quite right. Something was wrong with it, but my still sleepy mind couldn't register what it was.

I managed to coax my tow truck into the tight space at the back end of the Voyager and shut off the ignition. I swung my feet out of the cab, no heels—it was even too early for heels—and approached a woman wearing green hospital scrubs standing next to her vehicle. She was either really, really tall, or the new model was not the typical size of a minivan.

That's when it registered that all four wheels were missing. No tires, no rims, nothing. The axles were flush with the driveway.

"Your tires were stolen, I see."

She crossed her arms over her chest and gave me a brisk nod. "We've had a bunch of vehicle break-ins out here and I thought installing a security light over the garage would keep me safe, but it didn't work. Obviously." She stared at her Voyager, squat on the cement.

"I wish the dispatcher had explained that, because I can't tow a car without wheels." This is how out of it I was, I hadn't asked Axle to come with me or cleared the details with the dispatcher. It would have been nice to have my lil' cuz' to help, but I knew someone else who could. I said, "Let me call and see how soon another tow truck can get here." I hauled out my cell phone and called Tanner. When he answered, he sounded fully awake and said he'd be there in a few minutes. Nothing was a great distance in the small town of Spruce Ridge and there was no traffic to speak of at this time.

Tanner would collect payment, not me, but that was all right. My bank account was finally in the black.

That prompted me to ask, "Can you make an insurance claim for this tow? If you're insured for a crime, maybe the coverage will include towing?"

She perked up. "Good thought. I'll check with my agent. But I can pay you for the tow, then I'll find out if I can be reimbursed." I didn't bother to explain she'd be paying the other driver.

Within minutes Tanner brought his flatbed to a stop next to my truck. "Hello, Tanner," I greeted him. "Sorry, I should've moved my truck. Let me do that now."

"No, leave it there." He nodded to the stranded woman. "I'm Tanner Utley. We'll have your vehicle removed in no time at all."

She told him where to deliver it and that she needed to grab her purse and the keys to the second car in her garage.

After she disappeared into her house, I said, "So, I've never come across this situation before."

"I have. It's been happening a lot lately. I hope the police catch the thieves soon. Let me show you how to tow a vehicle with tires and rims missing. You need to use tow cradles."

"Are those like tow dollies?"

"You insert them into the dollies. The exposed brake rotors fit in the cradles which protect the rotors from damage and allow the rotor to fit into the dolly. Without it the rotor would not fit to lift and tow the vehicle. Go get your dollies and I'll get the rest of the equipment we'll need." Tanner's long legs sped over to his flatbed where he rummaged around in the hold.

I bent low to reach under my truck bed and released the two dollies from the undermounts. I also grabbed my hydraulic car jack and wood blocks.

He said, "We're going to chain the disabled vehicle's control arms to the cross bar of the boom and then dolly the rear tires with the cradles."

"Okay. Let's do it."

Once the jack lifted one corner of the car off the ground, I shoved the wood block underneath and Tanner released the jack. We repeated the procedure on the other side. We positioned the tow dollies under the place where the tires should've been. Then the expert tow man brought out two pieces of metallic equipment that I'd never seen before.

"Those the cradles?"

"Yes. The rotors sink into the pockets pretty securely, but you need to use safety straps, too." He slid the first cradle on top of the dolly and pumped the dolly up to where the cradle met the rotor. Then he ratcheted safety straps from the rotors to the dolly and eased out the wood block.

"Let me do the next one." It took me a few minutes longer than Tanner, but he must've thought I'd done a decent job since he didn't redo anything. Soon we had the vehicle ready to roll.

The whole operation had taken less than ten minutes thanks to Tanner. The customer had reappeared and handed me her credit card.

I pointed to Tanner. "He'll take the payment."

But Tanner shook his head and said, "No, pay her," meaning me. I didn't want to argue in front of the woman, so I gave Tanner a look to say *I'll pay you back* and ran her plastic through my card reader.

"I'm glad you're doing the tow." He added in a near whisper, "I want you to get a feel for how it rides," with a hint of a smile at the corner of his mouth. I flashed a look at my customer then a quick glance at Tanner, but let his comment slide. Was he flirting?

I fired up the tow truck and the rumble of the engine made my heart glad as it always did. I pulled the Voyager forward with enough room to let the customer drive her other car out of the garage. She sped off with a honk and a wave.

Tanner and I met at the back of his flatbed. "Hey, thanks again," I told him. "I had seven tows earlier tonight from Ridgeside Condos. Or last night, rather."

"You did?" His blue eyes crinkled at the corners.

I chuckled with deep satisfaction and explained about the rave party and the illegally parked cars. "Next time I'll call you to help. I didn't realize there'd be that many."

"If the party organizers are smart, they'll find another location."

"It looked like the police arrested somebody, so they probably will."

We stared at each other, and Tanner perused me from head to toe. I saw interest behind his baby blues. "I need to go." I couldn't meet his eyes.

"Text me to meet after you drop off the van."

"Okay. Then I can return your equipment." I felt his gaze on me as I walked back to my truck and climbed in. There were so many cheeky things I could have said about that, but didn't. *Na-uh*. Not going there.

I cruised across town and delivered the minivan to the tire store requested by the customer. It took me a lot longer to disengage all the equipment than it took Tanner to hook everything up, but I was happy that he trusted me to do it on my own. After I was done, Tanner and I met at the parking lot behind Roasters. Together we transferred his equipment to his flatbed and Tanner took off.

My phone told me it was five fifteen. No need to return my truck to the storage space at Oberly Motors since my work day was soon to begin. The sun would not come up for another hour, so I trudged up the steps to my apartment, padded through the kitchen to my bedroom, and plonked myself down on the bed. My eyelids were stuck shut when I woke up two hours later and rolled out from under the covers and into the bathroom for a shower.

Once my hair was dry, I twisted the strands into my usual braid, dressed, and downed two cups of coffee. I was finally ready for the day that had started hours earlier. I slung my purse over my shoulder and locked the door behind me.

Descending the exterior stairs, I caught a glimpse of the parking lot and thought I was still dreaming. I pushed my fists into my eyes to scrub away the fog and looked again. An oversized flatbed, not Tanner's, was backed up to my red self-loader, my baby with Del's Towing and the outline of a black stiletto on the door.

I shot across the lot and skidded to a stop between the flat bed and my truck. I yelled, "What do you think you're doing? Stop right there." I sounded just like the victim of a repo job.

DiNardo came around the far side of the flatbed. "Ms. Morran. Please step out of the way."

"Now you've gone too far." Rage reared up in me.

I'm sure I had on the look of a mama bear ready to fight a human who got in between her and her cub. "You take that flatbed and get out of here." Mack, one of the other towmen in town, stepped down out of the flatbed and gave me an apologetic look.

DiNardo said while adjusting his bow tie, "You still owe the IRS $1,284.36 per tax code §2.3104.141a."

"This is unbelievable. You would take my tow truck, a truck worth over thirty thousand dollars, for a measly thousand bucks." I was about to rip him a new one.

"$1,284.36. If you don't pay or make arrangements to settle your tax debt, the IRS can levy, seize, and sell any type of real or personal property that you own or have an interest in. I'm quoting the tax code. The truck is your only asset. And this is the only time your truck's been left in an unsecured lot. This is our first opportunity to seize it, or we would have taken it before now. Normally you store it behind that locked fence at Oberly Motors."

I pictured him bullied as a kid, and now that he had all the power, it had gone to his head. DiNerdo may be a nerd I could beat up in a fist fight, but he had the whole IRS to back him up and he was calling the shots.

I blew out a breath and flung my long plait over my shoulder. "You've been keeping an eye on my truck, so I'm surprised you haven't been watching my bank account more closely. If you had, you would've known I have the full amount." I even had more than that.

"You do?" DiNardo actually smiled. "That would be so much simpler. Think of the paperwork involved in getting the truck returned."

My imagination went to the Indiana Jones movie

when the government lost the Arc of the Covenant. No way the IRS is taking my truck. It would disappear forever. I told him, "Follow me to the bank and I'll give you the cash."

I jumped inside and fired up the engine with a roar. Mack had no choice but to move his flatbed out of the way. I rammed the truck into gear, mashed my stiletto to the pedal, and took off, laying down a few inches of rubber. But then I remembered the ticket and eased my foot off the gas. DiNerdo's Honda HR-V, front-wheel drive, followed me sedately down Pine Street to the bank on Main. With a final twist of the wheel, I slowed into the bank's parking lot and muscled my truck into a space between a Toyota Avalon and an Audi A4, both front-wheel drive.

"You're coming inside with me," I instructed DiNerdo when he got out of his Honda. "I don't trust you out here with my truck."

He gave his tie a quick tug, nodded, and followed me in. We were out of there in minutes since there were no other customers at the teller's window. Evidently, every other person did their banking online.

"Here's your $1,284.36 per tax code §2.3104.141a." I had asked the teller to count out the correct amount for me, so that I had the exact change, and I even got the exact citation right. "But you haven't heard the end of this. I'm still going to appeal."

Although I'd paid the amount in full and was soon to see the back of Nerd DiNerdo, I might as well try to figure out if I overpaid. Which I totally believe I did.

The tax collector placed the bills and coins into a canvas money bag and inserted the bag into his slim briefcase. He wrote out a receipt and handed it to me.

Then he slid into his driver's seat and buckled up. "Nice doing business with you." He waved before taking off.

I had a spring in my step when I headed back to my beautiful red self-loader. I rubbed my hand down the length of the metal and gave the bumper a loving pat. The smile on my face kept breaking out into a full-on grin as I enjoyed the moment. My self-loader was safe.

My attachment to the truck was easy to explain. It had been my dad's. When I climbed back into the driver's seat, I caught my reflection in the rearview mirror. I don't know what I expected to see, but the determination on my face boosted me up. This was just what I needed. I knew I could do my job, earn enough to pay my taxes and support myself, and that I would be okay.

With plenty left in my account to pay for the laptop repair, I drove over to the mall and made my way into the computer shop.

When the clerk processed my debit card and it actually went through, he mentioned, "Hey, I dug around a bit more and found out who was behind that computer virus."

I clutched the edge of the counter. "You did? Who was it?"

He faced me squarely. "You might want to make a complaint. It was another tow operator in town. Owen Eckerd. You know him?"

The shock rendered me silent. A couple of dizzy moments passed before I managed to squeak out, "Owen Eckerd?"

Yes," he supplied the answer. The man was in his element. He explained something about IP addresses that I couldn't quite grasp because I felt a sense of suffocation that somehow rendered me deaf.

When he retrieved my laptop from a shelf under the cash register, I thrust my hands out to steady myself.

"Are you okay?"

I was not okay. Not anymore. "I think I need to sit down." My heart rate had soared again, and my face was certainly bright red.

He led me to a stool behind the counter. I sat and tried to get my breathing back to normal. He handed me a bottle of water, then left to help a customer in the printer ink aisle.

I was really starting to feel put out. First DiNerdo, then Owen, had messed with me. I'd finished with DiNerdo, now I had to figure out what to do about Owen.

Owen Eckerd was trying to drive me out of the car hauling business. He must've thought a computer virus would cause me so many problems I'd give up driving my truck. Then, he'd get my piece of the towing work for himself. Ridgeside Condos would ask him to take back the contract to monitor the resident's parking lot. The city would call him in the middle of the night to handle their vehicle recovery work. Nancy Abington would instruct her repo agent Patrick Crump to call Owen whenever a vehicle needed repossessed. Yep, all that and more if I was out of the business.

But little did Owen know, I wasn't a real threat, at least I didn't feel like one.

No, I felt like an imposter, attempting to do a job I probably had no business doing. Strutting around in my high heels, pretending to be a professional vehicle recovery specialist. A business owner who couldn't even pay a measly tax debt on time because I didn't know enough to back up my thumb drive. I was such a loser.

Before I knew what Owen had done to me, I'd been feeling pretty good about myself. Not so much now. But I told myself, *enough is enough.* I stood up, trying to keep my ankles from giving out in these heels.

The clerk came back into view, so I told him, "I'm feeling better now," keeping my tone light.

"Are you sure you're okay?" he asked.

I forced my head up and down. "I'm fine." It was one of the best lies I ever told. If Owen Eckerd turned up dead, I didn't want the clerk to recall my red-hot anger.

Because I was livid all right. Furious enough to kill that ugly driver with the ugly green tow truck.

Chapter 19

I punched in the number for Owen Eckerd I'd found on the internet and left a scathing message. One that would make my mother blush and say, "Delaney, language."

After leaving that brilliant rant—so much for being discreet—I knew exactly where I was going next.

Not to confront Owen Eckerd, though, because I had no idea where he lived or where to find him. All I had was his phone number. I'd deal with him the next time I saw him.

I drove over to Spruce Ridge Accounting and slammed the door hard as I got out. Clark's files had been released from police custody and I had my laptop. Now, for the thumb drive. Once in hand, I could fight the IRS. And win and get my money back. I was almost sure of it. I was in a fighting mood, after all.

I should return to solving the murder, too, even though I'd have my flash drive back. I hadn't forgotten about Tanner, who never neglected to help when I needed him.

In fact, my mind was on the murder right now. After jogging through the entryway, I bypassed the front stairwell and proceeded to the back. Since the accountant's records had been returned, the crime scene had probably been released by the police, too, and the stairs would no longer be cordoned off. I was curious to have a look at the scene.

As I ascended the steps, I thought hard about the possible motives—money, love, jealousy—and there were plenty of suspects for each. I ticked the names off, one by one, except for Tanner who didn't qualify to be on the suspect list as far as I was concerned.

Dealership owner Nancy Abington, who'd lost tens of thousands of dollars, was out to dinner with her top car salesman at the time of Clark's death. Flower shop owner Anne Sullivan had a confirmed alibi, too, with her husband and grandbaby. Noel Yarborough had been spotted in his wine tasting room by a police officer during the pertinent window of time. Lena Fields, the kickboxer with a sharp temper, was teaching a class that night. Hailey at Friendly Finance knew the victim well, but had a solid alibi. The other suspect was Mike Horn with Main Street Coffee, but he didn't have a motive since he hadn't lost any money to Clark. The sheriff's department had cleared Clark's business partner, Megan Putnam, and former boyfriend, Grayson Thomas, by verifying their alibis. Which was too bad, because I had liked them for the crime.

There had to be others I didn't know about. Imagine that? Hard to believe I hadn't *sussed* out every single one of the possible suspects, *amiright?*

But I didn't have the complete client list. Without the list, I was still in the dark.

Someone's footfalls echoed on the cement treads. Someone else was in the stairwell. I was right. The yellow crime scene tape had been removed.

When I turned the corner to the top landing, there was Owen Eckerd coming down. Good. Just the person I wanted to see. I did my best to curb the impulse to run up the rest of the steps and punch him.

Instead, I said, my voice amazingly calm, "Hello, Owen. We need to talk."

He rested one hand on the rail and his other on a hideous purple carrier bag hanging across his belly. "I got your message. *Jeez*, Delaney. Language."

"You owe me an explanation." I gave him a *now-you're-going-to-get-it* look.

He sucked in some air. "What for?"

"You know what for." I huffed an outraged breath and climbed a few more treads.

The big man positioned himself under the stairwell exit sign. "Is that right?"

He didn't intimidate me. He was going to stay and hear what I had to say. I wasn't done, yet.

"That's right. You're not going to get away with it, Owen." I snorted to make a point. "I'm going to prove you did it, then you are going down. You're going to pay for this. Your little *trick*," I emphasized that word, "only made me more determined than ever."

His eyes narrowed and he clutched his carrier bag tighter to his chest. "More determined? More determined to do what? Prove I'm the killer?"

"Funny." He was going to pay for my laptop repair. And for trying to steal my customers and wreck my chances for success. I had no time for this idiot, so I continued up a few steps. But his heavy body blocked the door.

"She got what she deserved, you know that." His voice had a hard edge.

"What did you say?"

"Emery got what she deserved."

Bells going off! Ring-a-ding-ding. Hello!

It was his voice I heard at the Chamber of Commerce meeting; I recognized it now. He said Emerald got what she deserved. I could smell his sweat and his pheromones were screaming danger.

He was the killer.

Owen killed Emery.

I whirled the other direction to head back down the steps.

"Where do you think you're going?"

"To the accounting office to get my files." After I left the building, after I called the police, and after he was behind bars, I'd come back for my thumb drive. I cast a glance over my shoulder to find he was close on my heels.

"Don't go any farther, Delaney. Don't move. I mean it." He could easily pick me up and toss me like an old pair of shoes, so I halted on the narrow step.

With a hand steadying myself on the cement wall, I turned around, my eyes drawn to his purple carrier bag. "That's why you're here, too, isn't it? Because the sheriff released Emery's records."

"Yeah." He hitched his bag higher on his shoulder. Paper-crammed file folders stuck out the zippered opening.

He was one of Emery's clients. One I hadn't known about.

"Did Emery skim your account like she did the others? Is that why you killed her?" I asked, inching down a step.

"Nancy told me you were good at solving murders. When I ran in to you at her office, she said you would figure out who killed Emery. That's why I sent you the computer virus. To keep you busy, too busy to run your own investigation."

"I know you're the one who sent the virus." That was all I'd started out to accuse him of. Not murder.

"That and the anonymous tip to the IRS. I told them you had assets." He laughed. "That probably kept you occupied."

I tumbled that around in my brain. "How did you even know I owed the IRS?"

"I saw DiNardo chasing you down at the coffee shop. I sent you that virus, then I *sicced* DiNardo on you with the tip."

I tilted my head, looked up at the ceiling spotted with dead flies, then closed my eyes. "Hang on a minute. How do you even know DiNardo?" I opened my eyes wide. "I know. DiNardo was here in town to investigate you. Not a rich guy. You. You're the one. He was hounding you, too. That's how you knew him."

"He kept showing up every time I turned around. It didn't help that Emery threatened to report me to the IRS. That's all I needed since they were already after me."

"I didn't have any more assets. Other than my truck, anyway."

"Not the point."

"So, you didn't kill Emery because she stole money from your account? You killed her because she was going to turn you in to the IRS. Why? For cooking your books?" I made a guess.

"I didn't think she was a very good accountant because she was so cheap. She said she'd give me a cut rate for being a new client. I just needed someone to legitimize my books. I never imagined she would figure out I falsified my records."

"Yeah, she told me she'd give me a discount, too." That was one of the reasons I decided to fight the tax bill.

"But I had the goods on her. She was stealing from her clients. I told her she had to keep quiet about me, or I'd blow the whistle on her. But she didn't seem to care. That's when she threatened to call the IRS. Before she took it any further, I had to get rid of her."

"The government will catch up with you. Believe me, I know."

"They can't prove anything. At least not now." He lifted his carrier bag an inch then eased it back down. "That's why I came here for my files. I'm going to destroy them as soon as I get a chance."

Why was he telling me all this? Because one shove and I was a goner? Who was I going to tell once I was lying dead at the bottom of the stairs?

"You're wrong about something."

"What's that?"

"You didn't need to kill her. She made some mistakes. She stole from her clients. I doubt she would've reported you. She had too many of her own crimes to hide."

"That would've been true, but she told me she was turning herself in. The whole reason she stole from her clients was to appear more successful than she was. She wanted Megan's approval, don't ask me why. I guess Megan was always cutting her down. Emery was very insecure, but then she had second thoughts and was going to confess."

"So, you lured her to the stairwell?"

"I didn't have to. She was leaving and I was coming up, like you and I right now. She was headed out to her self-defense class with Lena Fields, she said."

So, that's why Owen wasn't caught on the surveillance camera in Clark's office. And I wished I had signed up for a class with Lena. She was a tough badass, someone who could protect herself. I could use a few pointers to help my escape.

My high heel hit the end of the tread, and I sneaked down another step.

Owen said, "I nabbed your flash drive along with my files. Nancy told me you needed it back, that the drive was your only copy, so I thought it might be useful." He held up the palm-sized drive with the label, "Del's Towing" taped to it. He dangled the thumb drive over the stairwell. "If I drop this, it'll break apart into little pieces. And there go all your records. Do you want to take that chance?"

"I couldn't care less." That was the truth. My debt was paid, and even though I wanted my money back from the IRS, it didn't matter that much at the moment.

Understatement!

And why was Nancy talking about me to Owen? Is nothing a secret in a small town?

He said, "I'm going to crush this thumb drive unless you come here and get it."

"So you can push me down the stairs like you did Emery? I don't think so."

He lunged forward and grabbed the front of my shirt in his fist. I was caught off guard, teetering on my heels on the edge of the tread.

I told him, "Let go of me."

"Say goodbye, Delaney."

"No, Owen. You say goodbye. Nobody's going to push me around anymore. Not even you." I stomped on his foot with my spiked heel, but he was wearing safety boots with steel toes. Unlike Grayson. I'd done some damage to Grayson's soft leathers.

So, I did what every other female in peril has done before me. I yanked on his beard since I wasn't above pulling hair, then I kneed him in the groin. You know what? Neither was as effective as I thought they would be. He grunted, then shook me until I was dizzy.

But I had another trick up my sleeve, what every female tow truck driver in peril has. What we all carry when out late on lonely back roads. *Please, please, please, don't let the canister be empty.* Another one of my inept moments as a vehicle recovery specialist had included an empty can of pepper spray.

Squirming around, I'd just about tore my shirt from his hold, and managed to poke my hand down into my purse, miraculously still on my shoulder. My fingers curled around a spray can.

"Ta dah!" I shouted as I hit the nozzle.

Owen had the full blast in his face. His hands let go of me and went to his eyes. We both coughed hard, so hard that we tumbled and fell, cascading toward the second floor landing. Bump, bump, bump, Owen laboring hard and me shrieking at each bounce. My nose was running and I was making pig sounds. I came to rest on top of his big fat body, which thankfully had cushioned my fall.

My eyes were watering like crazy. I pushed myself off him, my elbow sinking into his belly, and I just about gagged some more, because, *eew.*

That's when I noticed he wasn't moving. And that's when I got really scared. Had I just killed a man?

"Owen! Owen! Answer me." I slapped his face, hard.

He stirred and began coughing. I was so relieved real tears mixed in with the water streaming down my face. *Ha.* I had gotten to slap Owen after all.

I reared back and punched him in the nose several times. No, not really. I didn't. That was just a fantasy.

My purse had spilled out on the steps, so I looked among the bits of stuff until I found my phone, then called 9-1-1.

Chapter 20

Ephraim was the first to respond, and soon after him an ambulance, a fire truck, a couple of Spruce Ridge patrol cars, and several more sheriff cruisers. Owen was conscious at this point and tried to tell the officers I'd attacked him in the stairwell, but no one believed a one-hundred and ten pound redhead would take on a two-hundred and fifty pound redneck unless it was in self-defense.

The stairwell was once again wrapped in crime scene tape. Owen was strapped to a stretcher, subdued and no longer a threat. I was sore and tapped out from a waning adrenaline rush.

After Owen left in the ambulance, I followed Ephraim to the sheriff's station to answer questions. I was more than happy to recount Owen's confession. Maybe I'd feel more generous tomorrow, but right now it was sweet revenge.

After a lengthy wait and once I'd signed my written statement, Ephraim walked me to my truck. He said, "Well, you did it again. You managed to confront a killer."

Yeah-ez!

I asked, "What's going to happen to Owen?"

"The ER doctor already released him into the sheriff's custody and he admitted everything."

"He wasn't hurt? Did he at least have a concussion?"

"No. He's going to be black and blue tomorrow, just like you."

"So, what's next?"

"Eckerd's being booked now on a second-degree murder charge."

"What's that mean, second-degree?"

"The homicide occurred in the spur of the moment. Eckerd said he tried to revive the victim after he shoved her down the stairs. Evidently he's a trained paramedic. His training kicked in, but his efforts couldn't save her. She died instantly."

I rubbed my chin. "You know what? I think I knew he was an EMT. I remember something about that." Something from a long time ago. And what I thought was a medical bracelet on Owen's wrist was probably a paramedic ID bracelet. That made sense.

"I have something for you." Ephraim handed me my thumb drive.

"You found it. I knew you'd come through for me." I teased a smile from his lips.

"And I knew you wouldn't give up until you solved the crime. You worry me, you know that?" He entwined his fingers in my braid and tipped my head back. His lips landed on mine, lingering. When he released me, he said, "I've got to get back inside."

Once he disappeared through the door, I rushed my sore body right over to the computer repair place at the mall.

The plastic device had fallen three flights of stairs and bounced off the cement several times as it went, but the tech guy was able to extract my files. He even uploaded my tax and business records to cloud storage. After I got home, I called my stepdad Will and sent him the link. He assured me he'd ask a tax attorney in his office to review my records. I was not willing to borrow cash from Mom, but was more than eager to receive free legal advice from Will. Don't even say what you're thinking. I can see the difference even if you can't. No judging.

****

A week later, I was back at Roasters on the Ridge at my favorite table in the front window. Rain shimmered on the other side of the glass, making everything look like a black and white film noir. But at least it wasn't snowing. That can happen in May in a Colorado mountain town.

The shop looked spic and span and smelled of cinnamon and coffee, like it always did. Nothing smelled more comforting than Kristen's latest batch. The barista, Guy, buzzed out from behind the counter delivering steaming drinks to customers. Rain sprayed the coffee shop window and sounded like a sprinkler hitting the siding.

I was daydreaming about how I found Clark's murderer, so I was feeling pretty good about myself. Me, super sleuth and bad-ass tow truck driver. The toes of my shoes were propped up on the chair across from me, and I was trying to concentrate on entering my invoices—no more procrastination—when a man strode up to my table.

"Ms. Morran."

"Mr. DiNardo." I slid my feet to the floor. "Thanks for meeting me here. There's the matter of $4.83 you owe me, in addition to the $1,437.12 overpayment. That's a total of $1,441.95."

Can you believe it? The IRS made a mistake. Uncle

Karen C. Whalen

Sam owed me a refund, not the other way around. Okay, so it wasn't that much, $4.83, plus the payment I made, but I gave DiNerdo a triumphant *I-told-you-so* look.

I asked, "Did you hear? My dad paid some estimated taxes before I took over the business. His payments were never applied. How hard could that have been for the IRS to figure out? The money was all paid under one entity, Del's Towing."

"Um...." His oversized Adam's apple bobbed. "This was a highly unusual error."

"So, when can I expect to receive my refund?" I used my stern but friendly voice.

DiNerdo gave me a tragic look. "According to tax code §2.3104.141b, the remittance may take up to eight weeks." He turned on his heel and popped open a large black umbrella. "I must be off. Juliette is waiting for me."

DiNerdo scurried out the door, his umbrella bobbing as he ran. He jumped into his Honda HR-V, front-wheel drive, and Juliette, looking as glamorous as ever, gave me a smile from the open door.

Off they went. I'd probably seen the last of the unlikely couple.

Guy strutted over to my table. "I want to thank you, Delaney, for that tip you gave me. I'm going to work Friday and Saturday nights at the wine tasting room."

"You're welcome." I called over to Kristen behind the counter. "That's okay with you, right?" She nodded.

Guy asked, "Where's your sidekick, Axle?"

"He's picking up his new car." My throat constricted a little since my buddy would no longer need me to drive him around. "Good luck with that second job. It'll probably be a lot of fun." I stood and stretched, cracking

240

my back, tucked my laptop in my bag, and walked out the door. I didn't have an umbrella, and my hair frizzled in my braid, but the sun was already starting to break through.

I got in my truck and buckled up. Before I rammed my key into the ignition, I extracted my cell and called my mom. I couldn't put this off any longer.

She answered, "Hello, hon. Will told me about all your excitement."

"What's that?" I cringed. Here it comes. The call I'd been dreading. *I should move home. I should sell the truck. I should get a new job.*

"You helped the police with an investigation and you won a dispute with the IRS. I'm proud of you, Laney."

I'd have to thank Will later for the spin he must have given her. Just goes to show, most of the things you worry about never happen. "Thanks, Mom. I haven't seen you much lately. We need to plan a shopping trip."

She jumped on that. She was free next week and wanted to know if Kristen could join us, too. Then she went on to share some gossip about the neighbors and Will's partners at the law firm until my phone beeped with an incoming call.

"Gotta go, Mom. Another call is coming through. Shopping next week for sure." I picked up the call to learn a man was stalled on County Road 2. A Dodge Challenger, rear-wheel drive, on the side of the road. Had all its wheels on, I checked.

When I showed up a full fifteen minutes later because I drove under the limit, the man started in on me. "Where's Del?"

I extracted myself from the truck, flaunting my

stilettos. "I'm Del. I'm the high-heeled tow truck driver. You want a tow, right?"

He took in my pink-beaded heels.

"I get it. You're a man, but you need me to fix your problem today, so move out of the way." I'd practically grown a pair. I tossed my red braid back and threw my arms out. "I got this."

He said, his voice quiet and low, "I was only going to thank you for coming out. And those are cute shoes you have on, too. Real bad-ass."

Yes, you heard that right.

I'm back!

A word about the author…

Karen C. Whalen is the author of two cozy mystery series, the Dinner Club Murder Mysteries and the Tow Truck Murder Mysteries. The first in the dinner club series, Everything Bundt the Truth, tied for First Place in the Suspense Novel category of the 2017 IDA Contest. The third in the tow truck series, Eyes on the Road, won Second Place in the 2023 Firebird Book Awards in the Cozy Mystery category. Whalen loves to host dinner parties, bike, hike, and read.